Perpetual
Comedown

PERPETUAL COMEDOWN
First published in 2023 by
New Island Books
Glenshesk House
10 Richview Office Park
Clonskeagh
Dublin D14 V8C4
Republic of Ireland

www.newisland.ie

Print ISBN: 978-1-84840-848-7
eBook ISBN: 978-1-84840-849-4

Chapter 1 of 'Step One: Camish Spring, or, The Hovel Papers' was first published in *Queer Love: An Anthology of Irish Fiction*, edited by Paul McVeigh (Southword Editions, 2021).

British Library Cataloguing in Publication Data. A CIP catalogue record for this book is available from the British Library.

Set in 11/15.25pt Stempel Garamond LT Com

Typeset by JVR Creative India
Edited by Stephen Reid
Cover design by Jack Smyth, jacksmyth.co
Printed by ScandBook, Sweden, scandbook.com

New Island Books gratefully acknowledges the financial support of the Arts Council/An Chomhairle Ealaíon.

Novel Fair: an Irish Writers Centre initiative

New Island Books is a member of Publishing Ireland.

10 9 8 7 6 5 4 3 2 1

Perpetual Comedown

Declan Toohey

NEW ISLAND

For my parents

Why not say straight out what is in one's heart, when one knows that one is not speaking idly?

Fyodor Dostoevsky, 'White Nights'

Lies, ultimately, are food for the soul; one does what one must to keep out of the bughouse.

Lippen D. Verzgort, *That Clear Small Screw of Time*

Prologue

October 15, 2019

Z = NaN

At present I'm conflicted, for I've met an ungainly fork. Of many paths, many roads. In that shaded wood, moreover, which Simone Longford accurately invoked, and in which I have discovered there is a haunting and relentless echo. Worst is that I feel here I have become one with many people. That I am a soul shifting across several planes of existence. And yet, everywhere a savage emptiness stalks me.

After an arbitrary choice and a great deal of walking, I'm transfixed by a beech in whose bark is carved VS. No sooner do I absorb these initials, however, than a shoeless man rolls into view, as if on wheels. He dons green cargo shorts and wears a royal-blue tank top and prickles, weirdly, cover his skin. They are like thin ruby spikes, these indefatigable hairs; the bastard children of fur and thorns. He reminds me of the squirrels at which, long ago, I used to throw rocks, singing folk songs as I did so. But unlike the squirrels, he has a ginger bowl cut and a ghastly beard.

I will call him Your Man.

'An honour to meet you,' I say, offering my hand.

I don't know why I've said this; it's very clearly a lie.

But Your Man doesn't answer, doesn't shake my hand. Nor does he follow my gaze to his torn shorts, which, I see now, are speckled with mustard stains.

He scowls, mutters, spits, he blocks the path forward. The flesh of his cheeks bobs in waves and drones. Yet about him, all the same, is pure sex-glow assurance: that of the GAA-head shaking his Mooju. But they do not match, the vibe he exudes and his image as it is, and for this reason I'm intrigued as much as I'm confused. And when he finally speaks up, in a conspiratorial hush, I recognise him further, for he has the heterochromatic eyes – one green, one brown – of my mother.

'Are you lost, babe?' he whispers.

I fucking am. Behind me it's bare, save for a light snow and two pines, beyond whose needles a quarter-light twinkles. The tortuous path back extends indefinitely into the horizon. Into this grey, hazy tableau. After some time I ask where I am. The words resound four times, then casually die off.

Those of Your Man don't.

'You don't need to know now, babe. For the moment, just listen.'

So I do, and his crusty lungs wheeze like a faltering accordion. Hearing tobacco, I crave smokes, then I pat my body for skins though I know they're all gone.

'This is my land, Darren. And sound as you look, I need solitude. I really do. I'm only good at my job because it gets fuckers like you back to where you belong, and fuckers like me more time to be alone.'

A wet-cat of an air hounds the back of our heads. A smell of sausages blows in from who the fuck knows. Regardless, no longer buzzed, in fact rather sluggish, Your Man directs me off the path.

We come to a dirty, slanted hovel which heretofore was not there.

Inside it's cosy. Rocking chairs, a fire. Between them, a scuffed desk. On the desk are a shoebox, a stack of paper, a typewriter, an ashtray, pencils. By the far wall is a countertop on which are an electric kettle and a bag of marshmallows, a jar of rice and a box of tea. I hear what I think is the music of Rick Astley, but I could very well be wrong. Beside the TV, tapwater drips. There is a cramped bookcase whose authors are all obscure. No oven nor a fridge, certainly no washing machine. A circular window oversees the path hither. The cold disappears once Your Man closes the door.

'Plant yourself down, doll.'

He motions to the far rocker. Doing so, I satiate my curiosity and flip open the shoebox. I discover hundreds of cigarettes. The typewriter is a working Brother Deluxe 660TR Correction. When I look up, Your Man hands me a yellow Clipper. I light up, inhale, stretch out, exhale.

Given the circumstances, I should be terrified. But I'm not. I'm fucking rosy.

On the back of the door is a small piece of paper. For the most part it's blank but its boldened header reads: THREE STEPS TOWARDS ILLUMINATION. Your Man spots me eyeing it and laughs.

Peat bursts in the hearth as we consider speaking but don't. We chain-smoke, make eye contact, but eventually I relent.

'All right, chief. Give us the steps so,' I say.

Then he lugs a cheap grin as though history were watching. In spite of everything, he is rather beautiful. I don't want to learn his name lest it puncture his mystique.

'I thought you'd never ask, babes.'

And though the timbre of his words are peaceful, full of promise, a tincture of malice creeps under their every phoneme.

Z = 0

But I suppose I should account for how I got here, when and in what capacity, and why my equanimity hasn't entirely deserted me in the shaded wood.

Earlier this morning, I was at a desk in the Ussher Library, of Trinity College Dublin, pretending to work on a thesis titled *Existential Realism in Postwar American Fiction*. To the right of my computer was my frazzled copy of *Being and Time*, in which I have scribbled enough marginalia to constitute a book of its own, but which after a year I am no closer to appreciating. To my left was a collection of stories by Flannery O'Connor and, beyond that, a thermos of Nescafé instant coffee, black, with three shots of Jameson swirling around in there somewhere. On my mind was neither the wordliness of the world nor the humid drawl of O'Connor's South. It wasn't even caffeine. Instead, the students around me distracted me from my work, and on account of their tans, fake and natural alike, my mind turned to pumpkins and to the gourd family more generally.

Then I was reminded of Camland, whose spectre has haunted me for the past six years, and whose being is inseparable from the Cucurbitaceae family.

This, as I said, was earlier in the morning. As recent as an hour ago, maybe, though I'm fundamentally unsure.

Since my surroundings have shifted from the library to this wood, my perception of time has slowed down substantially. Here in the hovel, time runs slower yet quicker than it does normally. More warped and more hostile, it's no longer a system I feel I can trust.

And while we're on the subject – of time, that is – I should say I'm due to meet my supervisor in a couple of hours. Because of my whereabouts, however, I don't see how that'll happen.

But in case it does, I'll fill you in.

Dr Kenneth Connolly is your poster boy for all that's wrong with academia. In the world of higher education there are predominately two types of people: good researchers who are bad at teaching, and good teachers who are bad at researching. (The good-and-good type is hard to find.) But Connolly is rare for being both a clumsy researcher *and* an abominable pedagogue; a cretin so spineless that he deserves to be thrown under the nearest oncoming train. Such are my fantasies while he sits at his desk, adjacent to his shelves and their Library of America novels, as he tears apart my work for being beholden to a thesis that, if he's honest, is not as compelling as I think it is.

That I am not without my hang-ups has something, I'll admit, to do with the passing of Professor Moya Nolan, my former supervisor, in whose presence one could always expect erudition and wit, whether sipping tea in her office or skulling pints in Kehoe's. We met in September 2016 when I started an MPhil at Trinity; we shacked up as doctoral buddies in September 2018. She was marvellous company, and her editorship second to none. Trenchant, encouraging, helpful, rewarding. She was someone for whom I was willing to sacrifice my misanthropic streaks, mostly because she dangled before me a tantalising representation of the person, with hard work, I might one day become.

In February of this year, though, she was the victim of a freak accident. On her way to Birr, County Offaly, she skidded on black ice and slammed sideways into a pole. She was planning to surprise her parents with a visit. En route, she picked up a Battenberg cake and an apple crumble from Elite Confectionery. A classic, last-minute gesture of hers. But when the emergency services arrived, the baked goods were as crushed beyond recognition as Moya's winsome face.

While my thesis gets worse every day – all thanks to Kenneth Connolly – there are at least my Camish Thoughts. My procrastination, that is, from what the Irish Research Council pay me to do.

Yes.

The Atlantis of academia. My *real* work.

Camland.

That's what I was thinking about, earlier in the Ussher Library, as I stared at the gourd-faced students sitting nearby. Then I looked out the window at a windswept sycamore, whose rusty leaves seemed to be giving me the finger. How rude, I thought. But I didn't retaliate. Instead I got up from my seat and made my way to the stacks, where I quickly fetched a book.

But not just any book.

No.

I pinched a particular Irish journal, which popped into my head on account of the gourd-faced students.

I snatched *Dwelobnik*'s eleventh issue.

Now, *Dwelobnik* is an institution if ever the Irish literary scene has seen one. But I'm aware there are people for whom *Dwelobnik* means nothing, or inspires only images of Russian satellites and Croatian ports and wheat-chewing, overall-wearing, Irish tramps who consider themselves happy to dwell in the People's Republic of Cork.

So for those stray few, I'll elucidate.

Since its inception in April 2014, *Dwelobnik* has blended academic criticism and fiction with each issue. Editor-in-chief Olivia O'Shaughnessy has a faultless eye for realist stories that parody recent developments in Irish culture and society. But that's merely her speciality, of which the magazine seems to throw up more as time passes. One could find anything in *Dwelobnik*, anything at all. The unifying thread seems to be prose from Irish writers that's philosophically out-there in nature. Or that blurs the boundaries between fiction and non-fiction.

But there was another reason for my fetching *Dwelobnik* this morning.

I was looking for confirmation that I'm sane.

Hear me out.

Two years ago, a piece of mine was accepted for a special issue of *Dwelobnik*, from whose cover the Camish flag was *supposed* to beam forth. As the magazine's eleventh issue, it was to be called 'Camland and its Discontents, Or, The Narrative That Never Ends'.

Only it never materialised. Neither my publication nor the special edition.

It vanished, things exploded, and I never really got over it.

And while it's been more than two years since my piece was meant to see publication, public interest in Camland has neither waned nor increased. After all, it can't. Because nobody knows about it.

But I know I wrote my submitted piece. I know I sent it off. I know that almost six months later I received a congratulatory email of acceptance from someone who claimed to be Olivia O'Shaughnessy. But somewhere along the way I was duped. Where, I still don't know.

I'll find out, however. Of that you can be certain.

In any case, once or twice a week, I fetch *Dwelobnik*'s eleventh issue and I study the horrendous cover (a broken Rolex, around which are the names of four contributors) and I pore over the contents page and search in vain for my name. For the title of a piece that was accepted but never published.

And I've been doing this now for almost two years.

So yeah, call me crazy.

But earlier this morning the craziest thing happened.

I went to the usual spot and reached high above my head. I counted the titles. I knew from past experience that the Ussher had only two copies of Issue 11, both of whose spines were cracked from my opening them. And white, furthermore, in comparison to the monochrome cover.

But this morning my finger detected a *third* copy, whose spine displayed a black sans-serif 11. On seeing this, I felt my heart rate quintuple. What was more, the spine was pink.

Holy fucking shit, I thought. Holy exasperated lemon-noodle circumference ghost, I thought.

Like a Scalextric set, my thoughts whizzed around in neat figure-eights, to the point where I couldn't separate the car from the racetrack, the thought from the thinker.

But it didn't matter. I grabbed the issue and beheld the cover. It was the same from before, the same from six years prior.

It was a pink-and-black flag. It said, 'Camland and its Discontents, Or, The Narrative That Never Ends', underneath which were the names of four contributors, Darren Walton being one of them.

Mother of Jupity, I thought.

Then I beelined to my desk to peruse the issue in earnest.

I was shaking, you will understand, as I returned to my chair. I was the happiest I'd ever been, possibly the happiest I'll ever be, because all my sacrifices were finally paying off. At long last, I had my hands on the *real* Issue 11. On what, for clarity's sake, I'll henceforth call Alt-*Dwelobnik*.

I was elated. So much so I no longer felt real. I was above everyone in the library. An emperor, a god. Through my veins coursed the same blood on which Jesus's system once flowed. It was a fact. And so, to exercise my newfound omnipotence, I looked back out the window and this time *I* gave the finger to the sycamore leaves, those impertinent rusty cunts. But I quickly desisted when I noticed I was muttering and the nearby gourd-faces were throwing me disapprobatory glances.

Then I grounded myself to the moment, my surroundings, my books. I touched my Heidegger and my O'Connor. I took a sip of cold coffee, whose alcoholic content I wished I had made stronger.

And yet, I was more than a little scared. For what if I opened the journal and there was nothing inside, only a libellous message, such as 'Darren Walton is a spoon', over and over, for two hundred pages? Or worse: 'Darren Walton is a fork'? Or worse still: 'Darren Walton is a decidedly trivial and mould-ridden piece of unwanted cutlery who should never be used for the consumption of food, hot and cold alike'?

That would be terrible.

So terrible, in fact, that I'd rip off my clothes and weep there and then if it happened.

But I had to find out. I needed to know.

Was this really the same journal I encountered years before? In the Iontas basement with Simone and Maebh? While I was an undergrad at Maynooth?

And several incoherent thoughts later, I opened the journal and verified that it was.

To be frank, I was a little disappointed. Because as I flipped over the cover I expected a choir of schoolboys to sing a major chord. Or for the journal's pages to cast a golden glow on my beautifully chiselled face. And neither of these things happened.

Despite that, I *wasn't* disappointed to see that mine, the opening piece, was the same masterpiece I wrote three years ago on acid.

The sight was so beautiful, in fact, that I teared up as I read it, and when I finished it I thought to read it aloud to the gourd-faced students sitting nearby. The Ussher, I knew, wasn't the *best* place for them to encounter my work for the first time; the piece said nothing of the three-dimensional narrative, for example, my other hobby horse of yore through which I hope, one day, to secure academic fame. But there was also no better time to learn of Camland than the present.

So I stood and delivered the most stentorian oration the Ussher has ever seen, I recited the entire thing, and it went a little something like this:

A Brief History of Camland

Many years after the establishment of the Irish Free State, there came into existence an alternate Ireland called Camland.

Not so much a separate geographical entity as a unique cultural concept, Camland took its name from the opposite of Ireland: where Ireland was full of anger or ire, Camland was predicated on equanimity. Hence its name – land of *calm*.

After 2005, Ireland was no more. Towns, villages, cities, counties were radically renamed. Donegal became Bratoba. Gorey, Slopium. Maynooth, Slorn. And so on.

In Camland, everyone was free to do as they pleased. Everyone lived on an island where nothing was unusual and all things inspired wonder. Everyone was honoured to live by the gospel of Cian Scanlon, the chief signee of the Camish Proclamation, who devoted his life to the Camish Republic.

There is no limit to what this country can achieve.

May its future be as colourful as the blood of its past.

Long live Camland.

Here's where it gets trippy, where I remain unclear on the causation, the facts, the timings, the vibrations.

For when I looked up from Alt-*Dwelobnik*, I expected to see faces – bemused Irish undergrads; ecstatic American postgrads; a stooped, irate librarian shushing me from a distance, scowling behind a pair of half-moon glasses.

But there were no gourd-faces when I looked up from Alt-*Dwelobnik*.

There were no despicably rude sycamores giving me the finger.

Instead I saw snow.

And pine trees.

And a beech. In whose bark was carved VS. Over and over and over.

I found myself in this shaded wood, and thereafter in this hovel. Smoking cigarettes with a strange individual whom I'm loath to call anything other than Your Man, even if this Irish-ism doesn't translate internationally.

And the weirdest thing is that I feel a clear sense of delight.

Why?

Because I was right all along when I claimed, years ago, that Camland and the three-dimensional narrative will result in my fame.

Alt-*Dwelobnik* is proof.

So, no matter where I am currently, why *wouldn't* I be delighted?

Z = NaN

Less than delightful, however, is that I no longer have Alt-*Dwelobnik* on my person; it went astray during my sudden transition from Trinity to the shaded wood.

Which, of course, is a most impudent bummer.

But Your Man is at hand.

He scuttles peacefully before me, pacing to and fro, arms folded while the kettle boils and I swing steadily in my rocking chair. I've yet to verify if he's a friend or a foe. But he seems like a congenial fellow. Besides, I've never known a mean ginger, much less a ginge as callipygian as this one. He also has an adorable underbite that makes him look like a sperm whale. Or Popeye. Or a cross between a sperm whale and Popeye. And as everyone knows, those born with an underbite are among the most solicitous people you'll ever meet. So if anyone's going to help me locate Alt-*Dwelobnik*, it's Your Man.

'You are correct, babes,' he says. 'But not for those reasons.'

'Gosh. You read *minds*?'

He shrugs.

'An overrated skill.'

'Not at all. I'm very jealous.'

He swats away my praise, during which I decide to test him.

'Prove it.'

'You just likened my chin to Popeye's.'

'Good god.'

'And a sperm whale's.'

'Ah, wow. I'm sorry. It really is a delicious chin, is all I meant.'

'I don't take kindly to flattery, babes.'

'No, really. You could *model* that thing. Like, all over the world. Provided you shaved first. Then moved abroad, played your cards right. You know?'

'We're not playing cards, Darren.'

'No, we're … What are we doing again?'

He points above the door to the basic-as-balls sign.

THREE STEPS TOWARDS ILLUMINATION.

I almost forgot.

Then there's a kettle-click, and Your Man turns his back to make tea.

'This Illumination thingy-mahooley,' I say. 'Is it a game?'

'You could say as much.'

'I love a game.'

'I know you do.'

'Of course! The mind-reading.'

I flick my cigarette in the fire and lean to the shoebox, where I pillage another smoke. Soon Your Man hands me a fat mug of tea, the colour of Van Gogh's sunflowers, having doubtless intuited just how I likes me tay.

'Thankee, good sir. Shame we've no cans, though.'

'Later, babe. After Step One of Illumination.'

'Oh yeah? Gosh. What a time.'

'Truly.'

We clink mugs.

I hold my unlit cigarette in one hand, sip tea from the other. Your Man sets his mug on the table and loads a sheet of paper into the typewriter, which, like the Steps, I almost forgot about. To keep myself busy I look out the window, beyond which there's snow. The tree that engrossed me earlier, however, is no longer a leafless beech. Now it's a pluming cedar. And yet, on its bark are three VS etchings. 'Who versus whom?' I want to ask. And I wonder. But I'm silent because Your Man has just started counting on his gargantuan fingers, each of which is like a little rolling pin.

'The three steps towards Illumination are as follows,' he says. 'Tell your story. Address gaps in the narrative. Revise all the facts. Do these three things and I promise you'll be illuminated. Do these three things and I promise we can leave.'

To be frank, I was expecting more. These nuggets seem far from a revelation on which to base an escape from these parts.

'Fuck that,' I say. 'What about Alt-*Dwelobnik*?'

'I'll get it for you after Step One. After you successfully tell your story.'

He nods to the typewriter.

'On *this*?' I say.

'Correct, babe. Its ribbon is endless, so smash away and don't worry about the mistakes. And when you're done, I'll fetch you Alt-*Dwelobnik* and a whole *slab* of cans. Then I'll get you back to the Ussher for your meeting with Kenneth Connolly. As you're meant to, as you will.'

I mull over his words. It's a simple choice, really. If I want to locate Alt-*Dwelobnik*, I've no option but to comply.

'Delighted to hear it, babe.'

Then he leaps from his chair and swipes his untouched tea and pours it down the sink and heads for the door. Opening it, he reveals another angle of the cedar. It's huge, I see now, it puts those Californian redwoods to shame. How had I not noticed its size before?

'Where did you go wrong, babes? How did you get here?' he says. 'I'll be back soon with Alt-*Dwelobnik*.'

'And don't forget the cans.'

He smiles.

'Of course. Happy typing, darling.'

He blows me a kiss, the madman, then swivels and walks away. He paves a trail into the distance and I listen to his snow-patter until he's disappeared from view. The elements come blowing in, the unblemished pages flutter. I get up and close the door. I sit back down. I drink my tea.

Then I light a cigarette and tally my few options.

In this foxhole, it seems, I haven't a whole lot to lose.

So I do what Your Man expects of me and start typing up my story.

And as I do so, once again, I think I hear the music of Rick Astley.

Step One

Camish Spring
or, The Hovel Papers

Step One

1

Initiating the ruckus of this drawn-out affair was my discovery of an underground cabal at Maynooth University devoted exclusively to the discussion of gourds. A seismic event in my life if ever there was one. And yet, prior to its revelation, I must throw you some biographical nuts.

These nuts will be small and tasty to consume. For those with allergies, chocolate-coated crisps from Prince Edward Island, Canada, will also be available. But it should be known these latter delicacies are dwindling.

I have only five left.

Nonetheless, they are mightily sumptuous.

*

Nut 1.

Maynooth University is located on the north-eastern fringes of County Kildare. As far as I know, it's the only university on the island of Ireland that has a monument of the pope to its name.

Or *a* pope, rather.

He's dead now, John Paul II. The poor boyo.

On that note. An unusual number of people have died on the road hither. Am I to blame? Perhaps. Stick around and we'll see.

But Maynooth.

Maynooth is a college mainly for culchies, for mature students and layabouts, for Greater Dublin Area teens who aren't smart enough for Trinity.

And why didn't I go to Trinity?

A most perspicacious question.

Because at the time I didn't want to participate in Trinity's arcane rituals, about which I knew little, but which I imagined all the same would begin with the age-old question, 'And where did *you* go to school?'

As a result, it was to Maynooth I moved in September 2012, and to while away the evenings I roved about town, taking particular refuge in the university's South Campus gardens, under an avenue of moulting limes, where I crunched underfoot twigs and whistled folk songs by Nick Drake and, on a whim, threw a pebble or two at squirrels, just to see if knocking them down would give me a buzz.

It didn't. Not because I was a psychopath, but because I never hit my furry mark.

I've always had a measly throw.

Therefore, I remained buzzless.

Until I encountered Andrew Laird and his plethora of fucking gourds.

Nut 2.

Andrew Laird was no paragon of personality. No big-dick energy, little guile, less charm. But he led to Maebh Kealy, and Maebh to Simone Longford, and Simone to Camland, and so it's with Laird I'll begin.

When we met, he lived under absurd conditions. Absurd, that is, because the gamut of his waking seconds revolved around a literary project he'd never complete: his PhD thesis. When I enrolled at Maynooth, he said he'd complete it in approximately six months.

About this he turned out to be wrong.

Still, it was quite the sight to see, Laird's library grind. The horrific posture and sunken pose. The scowl in his usual seat. The tower of books by or about Thomas Mann. His HP Pavilion g6, whirring away at a distracting and chronic volume.

On what precise topic he'd proposed to whack out 80,000 words I can never remember. I'm sure he informed us during that infamous first seminar; something, maybe, about embryonic issues within the field of ecocriticism, about flora and fauna, or the role that they play in *The Magic Mountain* or *Buddenbrooks*.

Regardless, that semester would be his last, not for anything to do with the submission of his thesis or the completion of his *viva* – he would never get around to either – but because on Christmas Eve, of all days, the wretched sod went missing and was never seen again.

Ah, that first seminar! What an innocent time.

It took place in the Iontas Building, in Room 1.3, which was a contender for the most inhospitable seminar room in Ireland.

This had to do with the begrudging fact that only fifteen chairs fit around the room's oval table. And yet the beginning of each year saw at least twenty-three students in every EN151 seminar. Those who weren't early enough to secure a prime spot were obliged to choose a seat by the wall, on chairs whose plastic swivel rests made one feel imprisoned, and on which to take legible notes was a task fit for Job.

The room also had a pair of sentient windows, which opened and closed to suit their whims. No matter the weather outside, no matter how much you played with their tiny remote, they couldn't be persuaded. And invariably they operated on a temperature system at odds with ours. When we were so hot as to be falling asleep they refused to open, and when the exterior chill rendered it impossible to concentrate they declined to close.

The first Tuesday it was stuffy. All twenty-three of us were seated. My notebook lay on the table and my blue BIC biro – the sole pen with which I've permitted myself to write since I promised myself at sixteen never to use an Aldi or a Lidl or a Eurostore biro again – rested behind my ear.

I looked upon everyone and swore to out-grade them all. Those who didn't belong here, those disinterested and apathetic, those who'd learn but the essentials of academese in order to advance their teacherly ambitions, those rare few whom I considered my rivals – no one was safe from the wrath of my writerly conquest.

Hold up.

Important sidenote.

If I sound like a ponce, that's because I was. (Maybe I still am; the jury remains out.) But I can safely say now, as I type these words in the hovel, that my will to fame stems from a long-entrenched desire – eyerolls at the ready! – for my mother to really love me.

As for my father, Ger, fuck him. I care little for the prick after everything we've been through.

But yes, my motives are easily explained. Childhood Development 101.

Between the ages of three and six I bonked everyone on the head when I didn't get what I wanted. Girls, boys, relatives, strangers – everyone got bonked. I even exclaimed as I did so. 'Bonk!' I'd say, bruising their crowns. But one day my mother had had enough. I bonked a girl in a playpark, where specifically I don't know. But the girl was crying, bleeding, the works. My mother apologised to the father, who laughed. He said she had five brothers. She was used to it. Then my mother squeezed my hand and quietly dragged me home. My brother Nicholas wasn't born yet and Ger was at work, so the house was horribly silent, and because the kitchen and the living room were sparsely furnished, the reverb was sharp as scissors. Even whispers sounded like dropped forks.

Then my mother swooshed.

That's the only way I can say it. She swooshed off her old image as the loveliest of mothers – a woman in whose arms I could have lived long into adulthood – and disclosed to me an alternate identity I never knew existed, an identity simultaneously enchanting and revolting.

And following this swoosh, she threatened to send me to Tasmania if I bonked a single kid again.

Naturally, I was horrified. All I knew of Tasmania was Taz, the Tasmanian Devil, that incongruous Looney Tune with the spectacular ability to turn himself into a tornado at a moment's notice. Terrified, I complied. I became a Good Boy, I obeyed my mother's every syllable. I excelled at school and every extracurricular activity, just to ensure the retention of my mother's love. And to stay far, far away from the wicked shores of Tasmania.

And I haven't changed since.

I desperately crave fame, I want every titbit of attention I can get, all because I need my mother, Anne-Marie Walton, to love me.

Oh, Mam.

Why?

Christ, what a digression.

Please forgive my histrionics and my inability to stay focused.

In Room 1.3, I was saying, no one was safe from the wrath of my writerly conquest.

Not even Andrew Laird, whose smile was calculated, his coat a camel-hair tan. Thanks to the proficiency of my detective skills I heard he was English. But on account of my terrible knowledge of British geography I was unable to determine the particulars of his provenance. His demeanour recalled those of a spy or a pantomime villain; an unusual thought since I hated pantomimes and knew next to nothing about spies. I had left the last Bond movie so bored I swore never to watch another again.

'Welcome,' said Laird, his palms opening in greeting. 'Over the next twelve weeks you'll all become very sick.'

Mine couldn't have been the only eyebrow to arch in R1.3 at that moment.

'Sick, that is, of William Wordsworth, his poetry, daffodils, iambic tetrameter, and manifold forms of literary criticism.'

No one laughed at his joke.

The windows, however, creaked open.

Nut 3.

The tutorials were uneventful, their content routine. The same three spoke, same guy was late, same girl failed to print off her readings. It was just that. Uniform, disciplined, grey, the same.

But what wasn't the same were Laird's lapel pins, which he varied each seminar. I recorded them on the sly into my spiral-bound notebook, and on account of my terrific memory, I remember them even today.

There was a stag's head, a pride flag, a coffee cup, a cat, an aster, a goldfish, an apricot, Venezuela.

Venezuela was strange, it was just an outline of the country, and I never figured out why he had it to begin with.

But he also had gourd pins. In various shapes and colours.

And on the morning of his terrible introductory joke, he was wearing was a pink pumpkin.

*

Nut 4.

I must address the mammoth in the vestibule.

Yes – Laird and I had sex.

Once. Terribly.

Here's how it happened.

I was working at the time in Manor Mills Shopping Centre. At a kiosk called Humble Steve's Ice Cream, in the middle of the main drag, between an O'Briens Café and Elverys Sports. It was fine. I learned a lot. Like how I have a violent distaste for bubblegum ice cream. And that an alarming number of Maynoothians pronounce sorbet with a hard T.

But my sexcapades.

It was December, of a Tuesday, when I closed Humble Steve's and skedaddled over to Brady's, where I saw Laird at the bar. I ordered a Guinness and plonked down beside him and we talked shite for three hours. I didn't mention his terrible joke. But I listed off ideas for an essay I was writing. I was doing a lot of ruminating, I told him, on masculinity, femininity, androgyny, capitalism. How couldn't I? I was a first-year English major.

Laird was a good listener. He hummed at the right moments, sipped his Heineken during others. While I was mid-spiel I noticed he was wearing a blue pumpkin. But I said nothing about it. Not then, anyway. I ploughed ahead.

'So yeah,' I said. 'Mascu-femininity is effectively a platform on which the death of capitalism will eventually take place.'

Then he laughed so hard I thought he might punch me, and when he finally recovered he said:

'I hope one day you realise how silly you sound.'

Shortly thereafter we went outside and smoked the last of his Carrols; an odd choice for an Englishman. I binned the last of the cigarette and said, 'Well I guess that's that.'

Only it wasn't.

We shifted the faces off each other for a good minute or two, until he asked, practically gasping, if I wanted to go back to his.

And I did.

Laird was so far gone after his many Heinekens, however, that we no sooner started banging than he excused himself to vomit. While he was in the bathroom, I gave serious thoughts to fleeing. Later I would desert hook-ups with the impunity of an infant. But then, in light of Laird's retches, I found myself considering how he would feel if I ran away. So after some deliberation, I chose to stay put and brew tea.

The bags took what felt like hours to find. When I found them, I couldn't believe where Laird kept them.

They lived in an orange pumpkin.

Not a real pumpkin, of course – such a thing in December would be revoltingly mushy – but a petite plastic orb in Laird's fridgeside cupboard whose top came off to reveal some twenty teabags.

And though I couldn't know it at the time, this was to be first of many, many tangible gourds.

Nut 5.

After two cups of revivifying tea, I asked Laird about the pumpkins. We were lying on his double bed, I was looking at his LED lights and his posters of World War II novels. I had never known anyone to ever enframe the work of Graham Greene.

'What's with the pumpkins?' I said.

He laughed.

'There's nothing to them.'

'Really?'

'Nothing. I just love a good pumpkin.'

I saw from his alarm clock that it was getting exceptionally late.

'I don't believe you.'

He shrugged.

'You're your own man, Daz. Believe whatever you want.'

I hated it when people called me Daz.

So I left.

Nut 6.

We never said goodbye. After I jammed on my shoes and hobbled past his door – an alarming portion of which was chipped, as though clawed with a giant rake – Laird reverted to talking about his thesis. I think he mumbled something about mallards and Hans Castorp. Possibly I'm exaggerating. But I remember there was an animal, and that his ecological argument was as muddy as mine was on mascu-femininity. And that, of all things, he likened the gist of his thesis to an album by David Bowie.

'You know,' he said, gesturing, 'the drug one.'

It took me a moment. Then I said:

'*Station to Station*?'

He snapped his fingers.

'Precisely.'

I nodded.

After a pause, we waved so long in silence, and on my walk home to student residence I wondered whether Laird was telling the truth about his gourd pins.

And how a fucking PhD candidate pronounced Bowie as *bough-ee*.

Nut 7.

I don't like talking about Laird. But because I'm almost finished with him, I'll persist.

Most didn't learn of Laird's disappearance until after Christmas. It marked a first for the university, since no member of its faculty or student body had ever vanished before. A distinct and foul mood hovered over that January's exams. It lingered longer for me. I did little worth mentioning during the second semester that year.

But in February 2013 a service took place in the university cathedral, at which Laird's mother and father were present. They told us their son was meant to meet them on Christmas Eve, at Birmingham Airport. There his father Jonathan wore a double-breasted suit and a shiny black cap and held up, at the arrival gate, a sheet of paper on which was 'Andrew Laird, PhDunce'. An hour passed before he and his wife Kay began to worry.

Had he not disappeared, perhaps things would be different. Perhaps then I could discuss him and still be my jolly self. But his body was never found. And that above all freaked me out. It still does. Because where the fuck *is* he? Was academia to blame? Were gourds? Was *he* in on Camland? Was he depressed, kidnapped, what? Did he really talk about *The Magic Mountain* and mallards that night in December?

I'll never know.

What I do know is that if I hadn't slept with Laird, I would never have met Maebh Kealy, a second-year English major who already knew, that February, that she would be repeating second year in September.

We met at Laird's service. She sat beside me, complimented my patent leather shoes, which I told her I hated because their pointiness made me look like an elf or an ailing Dutch maiden.

'But that's a bitching brooch,' I said.

'Please elaborate. I could do with the praise,' she said.

'A purple dragon in a blue mitre? What's not to love?'

She told me in the moment that it was made from amethysts, sterling silver, sapphires, white gold. The following week we split a litre of vanilla vodka and she confessed that she'd been lying. She *actually* got the brooch for a tenner in Turin. And for the most part it was plastic.

But even now, as I stack these pages in the hovel, I'm not sure I can believe her.

As you'll see, she was as big a spoofer as me.

2

On a somewhat sad note, my nuts are all gone. Which means the time
has come for those chocolate-coated crisps from Prince Edward Island
I mentioned earlier.

You may have forgotten about them. If so, not to worry.

They haven't got any less sumptuous in the interim.

Chocolate-coated crisp 1.

Not only was Maebh Kealy the first chum I made at Maynooth;
she remained my most reliable companion during the three years we
studied there. I'm reluctant to call her my best friend, however, since
the phrase implies an intimacy that has few weak links, and in my case
no one has ever held this title for long.

Maebh wasn't one to make small talk. She spoke to be heard. To a stranger I once caught her saying, 'A good life is one in which our mistakes are not so severe as to deliver us to an early grave, a prison, a psychiatric unit, or a terrible marriage in which we've already had children'. I told the addressee that, interestingly, Maebh herself sprung from a loveless marriage in which her parents gave everything but affection. Then she ruthlessly backhanded me in the ribs.

This was how we typically conversed.

You could say she embodied the Hibernian Hipster. On her legs at most times were Kelly-green cords; sometimes she wore overalls. Her hair she unfailingly boasted in a neat and small bun, which accentuated the shaved panel at the base of her skull. To her petite ears and square-shaped face there were eight embellishments, namely nondescript piercings and circular glasses. When she smiled, she looked a tad like Elizabeth Taylor.

And, come to think of it, a smidgen like my mother.

Why is it only now that I'm seeing these connections?

I invoke the figure of Maebh because it was she who led me deeper into the strange and dangerous world of gourds.

Chocolate-coated crisp 2.

It's possible things went to shit before Maebh opened Pandora's Pumpkin.

My timeline, admittedly, is full of blips and elisions, so let me clarify while we're ahead and the mallards remain in sight and we can mow the bastards down with our buckshot-stuffed guns.

Forgive the incessant food-talk; I'm starving.

I said I first encountered Maebh in February 2013. All well and good there. What I failed to mention was that, concurrently, there was an altercation where I lived – in my three-bedroom apartment on the Maynooth University campus – between myself and one roommate whose disgusting and old-fashioned name I still can't bring myself to shout, type or whisper.

Was he in the wrong? Of course.

Was I? You fucking bet.

But whip your dick out after I've told you I don't want it and I will certainly fuck you up.

Which is exactly what I did.

Then I pleaded with student residence not to bring the authorities into it. Eventually they relented, on the condition that I move out immediately. I agreed. I was tired of living on campus anyway. My flat had all the ambience of a hotel room, with none of the attendant holiday sex. What was more, the rent was extortionate, and had my parents not paid the first three-months' outright, I would certainly have been fucked.

So I was happy to get out, happier still to find digs with a curly-haired Louth-woman whose name was Aoibheann Fagan. She lived on the far side of town, in Park Lane; a small estate whose green was permanently dishevelled. After a week I was so tired of raising my venetian blinds to the overgrown lawn that I went out and trimmed the entire thing, in my dressing gown, with Aoibheann's push mower.

And everyone in Park Lane was delighted with my efforts.

One neighbour even clapped as I pushed the mower home.

Okay, I lied.

Things *definitely* went to shit before Maebh opened Pandora's Pumpkin in November 2013.

What happened?

Well, in May I sat my first-year exams, then I went back to Kinnegad to work as a lackey at my father's practice. He's a solicitor. My plan for three months was to raise capital and read *Middlemarch* and smoke the occasional joint. To puck sliotars with my brother Nicholas and his ginormous fucking ears.

(Honestly, you should have seen him before the surgery; like a mug with two handles.)

Then my mother turned on me.

Yeah.

That's what happened.

Chocolate-coated crisp 3.

I first picked up on my mother's moods in third class, a couple of years after Bonkgate. I remember because at the time, threes dominated my life. It was 2003, I was in third class, I scored my first hat-trick in a competitive game of soccer, I learned of triads on the piano and the trefoil in our family crest, and I noticed that my mother had three main states of being. I called them Mam's Three Bs, though I never used the phrase in her company.

They were Beautiful, Bored, Busy.

It's not that they were horrendous. In the beginning, they weren't. But they were unpredictable. And that's what threw me the most.

On good days, following two bowls of Rice Krispies, she walked me to school and held my hand. We waved goodbye at the gates, where I admired her famous pink raincoat and her thin, caramel bangs. She crouched and smiled and rested her other hand on her knee.

These were the days on which she was Beautiful and I adored her every action and utterance.

But on days when she was Bored, she was uncommunicative, elsewhere, she frustrated me so much that oftentimes I cried. Not least because, on these days, my father walked me to school but the bastard never held my hand. And without fail when I came home my mother wouldn't leave her bedroom.

But one afternoon I crept onto the landing and into her room and I snuggled up beside her. She was wide awake but lifeless. She didn't move. She blinked.

'Are you okay, Mammy?' I said.

'No, Darren.'

She sounded like I did on rainy days, when I had read everything in the house and played *Rayman* for two hours and there was nothing else to do but watch shite TV and look out the window at the Mullingar Road.

'What's wrong, Mammy?'

She said nothing. As did I. And because I didn't know what to say, I hugged her. And on her breast was the sweetest tang I ever smelled, something like a cross between shin pads and strawberries.

Then she was Busy, which wasn't upsetting at first. If anything, it was fun. In the beginning.

To get me out of bed she might sing improvised rhymes. Or, when I went downstairs, I'd see fairy cakes and chocolate tarts and apple crumbles and Victoria sponges. All, of course, made during the night.

'A cake for everyone in the audience!' she'd say, then laugh for hours.

On the way to school she never stopped talking, observing, wondering. Once she dragged me into the grocer's for 'essentials' and we emerged with a party pack of crisps and fire logs and gobstoppers.

'I know they're not allowed,' she said, handing me the bag of gobstoppers. 'But sneak them to your classmates and they'll love you forever, I swear.'

Usually during these periods she was late to pick me up. And covered in flour and butter. She worked at the local bakery-café, mostly on the till. But when she was Busy she liked to work in the back because she loved using her hands.

My mother cycled through these moods consistently over the years; one followed the other as a ram might follow a ewe. But with each year, they became a little more intense, and occasionally she did something so out of the ordinary that my father smiled as much as he worried. Like the time she stayed up all night painting a series of portraits in which nude, dead Taoisigh spread-eagled in wing chairs, even though my mother, before then, had never expressed an interest in visual art.

We were surprised she managed to find supplies in Kinnegad at such short notice. We were less surprised that her paintings were far from good.

'Is that Dev or Jack Lynch?' my father said. 'Because I can't tell.'

Chocolate-coated crisp 4.

As with Laird, so with my mother. I don't like to talk about her.

How best, then, to condense the summer in which she turned on me? In tweets? As a series of Instagram posts? As a montage over which a frenetic, royalty-free, pop-punk musician – side-fringe smudging his eye liner – grieves over a jilting lover?

No.

I'll just tell you.

That summer I got my hands on frustratingly little weed. I threw basketballs. I kicked footballs. I discovered my thirteen-year-old brother couldn't puck a sliotar further than twenty metres. I slaved away in my father's office, I sent emails with many thanks. My father and I talked business and village gossip and horseracing, when all he really wanted to say, I know, was that he despised me and always would.

In the middle of which, I made my mother a gift and she hated it and, to punish me, she 'casually acquired' a pair of decorative gourds that she *knew* would terrify me.

In short, things got bad.

In July she was in the hospital for an especially doleful mood, so I made her a board game to cheer her up. It was flimsy but heartfelt. Assembling it was easy. I went to Dixie, an aspiring woodworker in the village, and I said, 'Dixie? I need a slab of wood, please and thank you. The same size as a chessboard.'

Then he fetched a square of walnut and I paid him and went home, where I drew four shapes on the slab – a circle and a triangle and a pentagon and a hexagon – in permanent black marker.

And with that Jupity was born.

I won't get into the technicalities of the game, it's an awfully complicated beast. But my mother was unhappy with the gift. In her hospital bed, she cried. And not in a good way. She looked at me as if I'd just torn up her clothes. She lifted the walnut slab and peered as if there, under this piece-of-shit board game whose pawns were twenty-cent coins, she might find her actual birthday present. She never thanked or hugged me. She just twiddled Nicholas's ears.

And not for the first time, I knew that I had failed her.

When she returned home a fortnight later, she brightened momentarily, even if she referred to the board game euphemistically as 'my effort'.

'I admire your effort, Darren, I really do. We'll have a game?'

So we did.

And we had a blast. The whole family. Only as the days went on and the household joking kept circling back to 'my effort', I realised that all of them hated it. That they were laughing at me and they thought I was worthless. And though I long knew my father harboured this opinion of me, it was shocking that my mother and Nicholas believed it now too.

Didn't they know I made Jupity out of love?

Evidently not, for once I noticed this purulent hatred of theirs I saw it everywhere in the house. In the fridge, the bathroom, the utility room; in their rearrangement of the condiments; in their soap-crusted razors; in their mugs whose tea and coffee stains sometimes resembled elephants, other times laughter emojis. Our dishwasher was out of action then, and because I take significant pleasure in plunging my hands in hot water and lathering up a storm, I was chief dish-scrubber for three months.

Their hatred was so ubiquitous that, by August, I couldn't stand it. Nicholas intentionally got worse at hurling, just to spite me during our nightly puckabouts. Ger became friendlier at work for similar reasons. He bought me doughnuts and coffee and a new book from Mullingar. But I could tell he was just doing it as the sneakiest of ruses. He was crafty.

But the most painful response was my mother's. She blanked me at all times, because nothing I did could ever meet her standards. I tried everything. I bought her tiger lilies, made her spinach and mushroom risotto. I wrote her a poem in heroic couplets, I did her laundry and no one else's. I ironed her clothes. I chopped the veg. I went to the ISPCA and adopted a basset hound, with floppy ears and dissipated eyes, and when she said, 'But petal, you *know* I'm allergic to dogs,' I dutifully took it back, much to the disgust of the ISPCA.

Then she brought home these gnarly gourds from a garden centre in Killalea and plonked them on the island and said, 'Aren't these the cutest things you've ever seen?'

And I screamed.

'I know what you're doing, Mam!'

'Lovey, what are you talking about?'

Then she tried to hug me, but on account of the gourds I wouldn't let her.

The three of them turned on me. That's all that matters.

Over what? A board game? Gourds?

No.

I suspected it ran deeper than that. It had to. But because I was due to return to Maynooth for my second year of undergraduate studies, I couldn't undertake further investigation. I'd have to wait until later to verify why and when and where and with whom my family really began to hate me.

But on a brighter note, I moved in with Maebh that September.

*

Chocolate-coated crisp 5.

Maebh and I lived above a Turkish barbershop, in the tiniest apartment I've ever known. She christened it Tiny Palace by pouring a drop of Babycham on the linoleum. (I received my primary education in drinking at the School of Maebh Kealy; it was one of her life goals to sample every drink in Ireland and so she always had a new beverage to offer me in the evenings.) The bedroom consisted of two twin beds and a shared dresser-cabinet. Our clothing rails were exposed. The kitchenette fridge was as tall as our waists. The water closet lived up to its name. In fact, the apartment wasn't much bigger than the hovel in which I sit now and stack these riveting pages.

And, never one to reassure a neurotic soul, Maebh told me I was crazy.

'You know I'm right, sunshine. I always am,' she said. 'Because think about it? You made a stupid board game for your family and what happened?'

She was drizzling golden syrup on a sizeable mound of pancakes. A staple of hers for dinner.

'Your mam didn't like it, that's it, nothing more. So what do you do next?'

She spread her syrup around her pancakes with Napoleonic intensity. The same intensity, I imagine, with which Francis Bacon painted his portraits. I wanted to get a word in but I had already talked for hours, and now that Maebh had the reins she wasn't letting go.

'You move on, sunshine. That's what. You hear me?' She jabbed her knife in my direction. 'You don't see symbols in your mayonnaise or read dinner plates like tea leaves.'

I said nothing.

'Now open that bottle of Dubonnet and let's pretend we're the fucking queen.'

I complied with her request while she forked the first of her pancakes.

Then we got belchingly drunk on Dubonnet sodas and lime.

3

Now that my crisps have been depleted, there's nothing left to do but dive straight for the heart of Camland.

To revisit Pandora's Pumpkin.

Let's go.

In the basement of the Iontas Building on Maynooth's North Campus were rows upon rows of enormous filing cabinets. They contained the papers of students past. Glaringly white, the room was reminiscent of the hospital in *The Grudge*. Maebh said that if you spent too much time down there alone, the silence and brightness began to play tricks on your mind.

But it wasn't for this reason that students stayed away from the basement. Rather it was because they were unaware of its existence. Maebh only knew about it on account of her uncle, a former academic whose eminency was undone at the pull of a button – or many buttons, I should say – and she wanted to prove to me she wasn't making it all up.

To access the basement, you passed through the emergency-exit doors at the end of the Iontas lecture hall. There you kept going until you met another door, above whose handle was a small blue circle that said, 'Fire door – keep shut'. Ignoring this order led you to a darkened stairway and, after that, the spooky basement of which I speak.

And for all I know, it may no longer be there.

Maebh and I only intended to have a gander. She said it was the coolest place on campus, after the room in Rhetoric House in which blood once dripped from the ceilings, and on whose demons a Californian priest ultimately performed an exorcism. She insisted on showing me herself.

And never one to believe her, I tagged along just so I could point out the errors of her judgement.

Such is the way many discoveries go.

You might think that, to start a cabal, you have to centre its organisation around something more compelling than the Cucurbitaceae family. But you'd be incorrect.

There is much to know of gourds, and much of interest to boot. Most express surprise to learn there are almost 100 genera within the family. Happy is the child who uncovers that, from gourds, one can make birdhouses, bottles and musical instruments. Some common examples of species and genera are:

Lagenaria – calabash. *Citrullus* – watermelon. *Cucumis* – cantaloupe. *Cucurbita* – pumpkin.

But during our prowl in the main basement room, no gourds littered the floor. No cucumber nor squash dwelled in a cabinet. But emanating from the anteroom – which prior to further exploration we never knew was an anteroom – was quite the discernible and obstreperous ruckus.

We followed the noise to its source, and I still wish partly that we had not.

The anteroom was bland and bare, the same size as classrooms in the John Hume Building – large enough to hold fifty or so students. It looked like a showroom more than anything else. Or a place where ballerinas danced, minus the handrails. There was a clear echo. It had no furniture. The walls were cadmium yellow. On them were posters of various gourds, along with a stencilled sign that said GOURD CITY, in the shape of a rainbow. In the corner idled a small garden patch.

More alarming was that in the centre of the room, dressed in wellington boots and a quilted gilet – the unquestionable trappings of your average Irish farmer – was Simone Longford, my seminar leader for that year's History of Ideas module. I turned to Maebh to see if she recognised Simone, but she never made eye contact: she only looked at my hair as though terrified by it. Immediately I became insecure. I licked both of my palms and rubbed the crown of my head. It was true that the edges of my skull were a tad like devil horns, as I hadn't showered that morning.

Then I looked back at Simone, whose get-up confused me because she didn't live on a farm. She lived in a housing estate – she told us as much during a recent seminar on Machiavelli. As for the attire we associated with her classes, she wore tweeds, boat shoes and rose-pink lipstick whose shade was so light as to be almost unnoticeable; she painted and bejewelled her nails differently each week, and on this occasion they were emerald green, with three obsidian studs. What was she doing in *wellies*?

Given the sartorial prowess she invariably exercised, I was unprepared to see her dressed for making silage.

But she, it seemed, was prepared to see us.

'Maebh; Darren!' she gushed. 'Care for a gourd?'

From her jacket pocket she removed a plastic tub and proffered it to us. In it were diced cucumber and cantaloupe. Though I wasn't a fan of either, I spooned out a handful and made sure, in the process, to thank our host. Maebh politely declined. I couldn't help but feel she was absent from this interaction. Why wasn't she as surprised as I was to meet Simone under these circumstances?

'The Australians call it rock melon,' Simone said, pointing to my cantaloupe. 'How do they taste?'

'Juicy,' I lied. They were as dry as the room in which we stood.

I stared at this woman – a trans woman, for what it's worth – whom I knew to be an entertaining and intelligent speaker. I was perplexed by her appearance, bewildered by her remarks. Why was she here? Why were *we* here? Why was my life so populated with gourds? This wasn't the woman I knew. Then again, after just a year in her company, a year in *classes* no less, I was foolish to think I could know her at all. It was transparent I didn't know her from Eve.

But I was curious.

'Why the gourds?' I said.

'They run the world, Darren.'

'Gourds?'

'Yes. See?'

Raising a vertical hand as though blessing us, she tugged down her shirt sleeve to reveal the corner of her wrist, where I saw a pink tattoo that faintly resembled an hourglass. I'll do my best to draw it now:

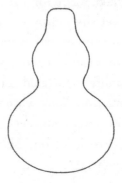

'Is that a pear?' I said.

'No, silly. A calabash.'

'Ah.'

'Also known as a gourd-bottle.'

I chewed on her words. Then I gave in and said:

'Yeah, I really don't see how that makes gourds run the world, Simone.'

She sighed.

'One day you will, Darren. For now, just know that the cantaloupe is the national fruit of Camland.'

'Okay?'

'And that there's no need to be afraid.'

I would have gulped had the air not been so arid. What the fuck was Camland? Why might I be afraid? The rapidity with which reality was slipping away from me was worrying. I reminded myself to breathe. Then I mused some more on her words.

'So why, in that case, don't you have a *cantaloupe* on your wrist?' I said.

She looked around the anteroom as if at an invisible audience.

'What foresight! What logic! That's why you're going to go far, Darren. That's why you'll be the first.'

'To … ?'

She scoffed.

'To bring Camland to the masses, silly!'

I ate another piece of cantaloupe because there was nothing else I could do.

Once more I looked at Maebh. This time she *was* in a trance, dancing ever so slightly with her shoulders and knees and wrists. Meanwhile, her eyes glanced at everything in the room save for me or Simone. Her stupor was so bad I wanted to bonk her on the spot, to bring her out of her daze.

But I didn't feel comfortable doing that in front of Simone.

'Look,' Simone said, 'the ringleaders of this club have told me I'm to issue a few warnings before we get started. I'll do my thing, then leave you to it. Sound gourd?'

We said nothing.

'Very well.'

She coughed a bone-razing bark, then rummaged around in the pocket of her shite-dyed jeans and retrieved a small and brittle pamphlet on whose cover was a triangle. Clasping it into Maebh's hands, she conducted this conveyance with a twinge of sadness, after which she lightly slapped Maebh to secure her attention. She succeeded. Then she said:

'The antics of John Heffernan McDonagh cannot be dismissed as a result of his obsession with the occult. Although this pamphlet is brief, Maebh, you'll find that his case was vastly more complicated than any essay in *The Cambridge Companion to J.H. McDonagh* will have you believe. In his story there are no easy answers, no straightforward conclusions. But the more you dig into the history of Maynooth University's founder, the more the coincidences will begin to make sense. I trust you'll not only interpret his doings in a novel light, but will elucidate for others how and where and when he went wrong, and what lessons we might learn from his nasty, brutish existence.'

When she concluded this speech, she turned to me and said:

'You, conversely, have more baggage to tow, more labour to front. But this too won't be without its reward. You'll find yourself in a shaded wood. But if you begin to prepare now you can escape with your sanity. You have time yet to put together a map, as it were, and get your utensils in order, so that when the time comes you'll be ready. Strong, even. Come.'

She jerked her head to the corner of the room, in the direction of the measly garden patch in which a few shoots protruded from underneath the soil. We shuffled over and hunkered down. Then Simone sunk her right hand in the dirt and emerged, after some struggle, with a book whose cover was emblazoned with a pink-and-black flag.

She handed it to me, I dusted off the soil. It had the weirdest name. Whatever it was, its publication date was ahead of us by four years. 'Autumn 2017', it said. Stumped, I turned over the cover and saw a list of contributors. I learned the book was a literary journal. I skimmed the names.

David Grierson, Lorraine Flanagan, Noelene Mulvihill, Sharon Ní Dhomhnaill and, of all people, Darren Walton.

Me?

I felt a sweat claw my skull. My throat flushed. I flipped the journal over once more.

Dwelobnik, Issue 11: 'Camland and its Discontents, Or, The Narrative That Never Ends'.

I responded in the only way I knew how.

'What the actual *fuck*, Simone?'

Yes, children.

Alt-*Dwelobnik*.

The very fucking thing-in-itself.

But back then there was nothing alternative about it. It was just *Dwelobnik*. Even though the first issue hadn't been published at the time.

This was November 2013, remember. Olivia O'Shaughnessy didn't launch the inaugural issue until April of the following year. So how could the *eleventh issue* of a quarterly magazine be available in 2013?

I don't know.

It's impossible.

And yet, it fucking happened.

But crazier is that this very morning – even if it already feels like years ago – I was finally reunited with Alt-*Dwelobnik*. After almost six years. In the Ussher Library of Trinity College.

Crazier still: that when I opened Alt-*Dwelobnik*, my surroundings shifted from the Ussher (and its despicably rude sycamores) to the shaded wood Simone prophesied in 2013. To Your Man's tiny hovel, where, though cosy and warm, I'm a little suspicious of what's to come when I finish telling my story and I complete Step One of Illumination and Your Man returns with Alt-*Dwelobnik*.

But who died and made Simone the soothsayer of Maynooth? How could she have known so much? What else was she hiding?

I don't know.

All I know is that if I want to leave this wood with that renegade issue in tow, and to also be on time for my meeting with Kenneth Connolly, then I must heed Your Man's words and continue telling my story.

So, back to gourds.

I opened the journal to its table of contents. Mine was the opening piece. 'A Brief History of Camland'. But no sooner had I flipped over the page than Simone made a lunge: she snatched the book from my hands and tossed it back on the soil.

'I can't let you do that,' she said. 'You'll write this piece on your own time, through your own investigations. Just as Maebh should put together an exegesis of the Slorn Sasquatch, so you should devote your attention to the study of Camland. Which believe you me, future generations will be *howling* to see.'

Maebh and I hadn't a clue what she was talking about. Slorn, a sasquatch, Camland – the jargon blundered forth with such abandon that the only thing to do was let it pulverise our faces. Curiosity gave way to alarm, intrigue to fear. Maebh was more with it now, more clued in. She was no longer shimmying. I could tell that she, like me, was beginning to question Simone's mental faculty, which heretofore I thought was immaculate and sought to emulate. Now I wasn't convinced.

'You're not convinced,' Simone said. 'Why don't I research Camland myself, right? A terrific question. Well, the answer is that I'm not in a position to.'

She cleared her throat with such force that I thought she might vomit.

'The answer is I'm dying.'

'Simone?' I said. 'That's terrible.'

We group-hugged.

'Thank you, my pretties. You're young, however. Able. I won't be here much longer. The world of Websitehawks, Darglar, Fairytop is not one I was born to inhabit, much less one I was meant to design.'

I considered these neologisms and wondered whether they were people, places or things. And if Simone was actually dying.

Seeing that I was daydreaming, however, she clapped her hands in front of my face.

'But if you want to write about a vital topic, Darren, and become the career researcher you claim you were born to be; if you want to isolate an untrammelled era in history, a moment in which society and the humanities fuse into one, and to disseminate this moment to the masses, then you'll contact Cian Scanlon, a History lecturer here at Maynooth. He also helms the university Writing Centre, so before you begin your project in earnest he'll be able to banish your bad writing habits. Of which, judging from your essay I recently corrected, you have many.'

Following this slight I can't say for sure what happened. I think the corner of a poster fell off. A laminate of a buffalo gourd, perhaps, its Blue Tack sweaty in the underground heat. Maybe Maebh started shimmying again.

Either way, I zoned out.

Ever since I was a child, I had seen the world as an extension of my dreamscapes. But where other people were typically the tether by which I established *some* connection to reality, now it was the reverse. Simone was no longer my teacher: she was a cross between a bridge troll and a magical elf, though one without pointy shoes. She had foregone her agency as a Maynoothian scholar, for her sole purpose, it seemed, was to propel Maebh and me on separate adventures. I felt a bad trip coming on and knew I needed fresh air.

So we parted.

I trust Simone changed her clothes. And more likely showered. Maebh and I, on the other hand, didn't speak about what had happened as we made our way upstairs. It was too soon, we intuited, and quite possibly too traumatic. What the fuck were its implications? Did we both experience the same thing? Could we agree on its particulars?

I knew we'd debrief later, over sake and lychee-liqueur, so I wasn't overly worried. I went to the bathroom and splashed water on my face, held the door open for a GAA-head in a Kerry or a Meath jersey. He thanked me with his eyebrows. He was real, *I* was real. What happened in the basement was obviously real. But when I came out of the men's rooms Maebh wasn't there. I waited outside the women's toilets for ten minutes. Then I gave up. There were two hours until our poetry lecture. I'd see her there or I wouldn't.

Meanwhile, I pushed out onto the Iontas forecourt, where a bronze orb of tessellated polygons sat in a pool of shallow rainwater. The water never disappeared, even on hot days. The orb was similar to that outside Dublin's Central Bank, only it looked like an apple from which a giant had taken a bite. I passed by the artwork every day and still I didn't know its name or artistic intentions. But at that moment I didn't care. I was outside and grateful for the wind whipping my face. Then I walked for the South Campus gardens, where I gave considerable thought to throwing rocks at squirrels. But I resisted my poorer judgement.

Later in JH1 I didn't see Maebh. I looked around the lecture hall and saw three hundred feckless faces. I trudged up the stairs and sat down at the back, where I failed to focus on an overview of Terry Eagleton's criticism. So I scribbled moody couplets to vent my hodgepodge emotions, but I couldn't tell if I was anxious, angry, excited, confused, ecstatic, serene, disgusted or surprised.

By the lecture's end, however, I concluded three things.

I wasn't a fan of Terry Eagleton, sonnets were not my creative forte, and no matter what Simone said about the quality of my essays, I would never seek help to improve my academic writing.

Fun fact.

It was February 2014 when I contacted Cian Scanlon and asked, with great shame, if he could help me improve my academic writing.

4

I'm getting ahead of myself, however.

Lots happened between November 2013 and February 2014. But meeting Scanlon was the accelerant. I can't yet say if he was the beginning or the end of me, my saviour or my Satan.

But I will say that he knew frightfully little of gourds. And he didn't have the tattoo. Even *I* have the tattoo. Both on my wrist and as a tramp stamp. One in pink, one black.

It's strange. Since that peculiar meeting in Gourd City I've seen the tattoo on more than one wrist. And yet I've never wrangled out of anyone a confession that, yes, they are card-carrying members of the Cucurbitaceae Club. Or citizens of Camland.

But I'm confident that Alt-*Dwelobnik* will clear everything up. Once Your Man eventually returns with it.

I know it will.

I was alarmed, you can imagine, as I walked home from my poetry lecture that blustery November evening, balls deep in gourds.

Had Maebh already imploded due to the pressure of Simone's words? Was she already floating face down and blue next to the swans and the bulrushes on the Royal Canal?

I couldn't say.

But as I walked towards Tiny Palace and saw a long row of traffic – the sharp red of the tail lights losing their vitality in the autumn grey – I blamed the weather for my anxiety.

November in Ireland isn't a fun time for anyone. Ask the Scorpios and Sagittarii born then and they'll tell you. The trees become naked, the wind cranks itself up. The clouds are never anything but low and impenetrable. It rains for the most part in every direction. It would rain up if it could.

But at Tiny Palace, there Maebh was. Taking vol-au-vents out of the oven.

'The man himself,' she said.

'Your one.'

'How's tricks?'

She closed the oven door and placed the tray on the grimy range. Beside it was a pot from which a yellow ladle poked its handle. Inside the pot, I assumed, was the creamiest of diced chicken.

'No poetry?' I said.

'Nah. Any good?'

She stirred the pot's contents before making the first scoop.

'It was all right,' I said.

'So … shite.'

I shrugged.

It *was* chicken, I saw, as Maebh crammed the nearest vol-au-vent, then flattened its contents down with the back of her plastic ladle.

But why hadn't she said anything about Simone, gourds, Camland, J.H. McDonagh, the sasquatch, the basement? What about her shimmying? Why were we conversing in platitudes?

I was too afraid to ask, so I watched her fill eleven vol-au-vents in silence, as my raincoat and jeans dripped water onto the lino.

Gosh.

The elevens were everywhere.

'Are you *okay*?' she said later.

Our dinner plates were empty and we were drinking Dutch Gold. I didn't remember sitting down. Or eating my dinner. And I could have sworn, moments previously, that I'd made us both mai tais.

Then I asked the necessary questions and got distressing results in return.

'An underground *cabal*?' she said. 'For *gourds*? In the Iontas basement?'

I got up for another can.

'You really don't know what I'm on about?'

Then she laughed so hard I had to turn away from our fridge, from the globe of sad lettuce and the half-full drawer of Dutchie.

'Do you really think I'm adventuring for a sasquatch?' she said.

I fetched us both a can and went back to the table and handed her hers. I cracked mine and became reticent. She tried to coax me from my hole with the promise of a movie. She had bought a TV recently for fifty quid on DoneDeal. It was on the wall opposite our beds and sometimes when we watched films, we reached out and held hands and, in our respective twin beds, pretended we were a couple in a 1930s screwball comedy.

'Cheer up,' she said. 'You're grand. Have a shower while I wash up, then we'll get stoned and watch *Clifford*.'

I mumbled something non-committal yet vaguely consensual.

'Martin Short as ten-year-old boy, sunshine. What's not to love?'

I said nothing.

'He was forty when it was filmed, Darren.'

She let the actor's age sink in.

'*Forty*. We'll have a ball.'

But we didn't. Our weed was heavily sprayed and I tripped harder than I would have liked. I thought Maebh was an actor incapable of true expression. All she could do was deliver her lines. I suspected she was lying and that even Martin Short's Clifford – with that awful, impish leer of his – was in on Gourd City too. But whom were they representing? And who were the 'ringleaders of this club' that Simone mentioned hours earlier?

Halfway through the film Maebh fell asleep and so I took to googling my new dramatis personae. On the internet I learned that Maynooth's founder wasn't J.H. McDonagh. It was some other dead white male whose name I can't recall. Worse, there were no books on McDonagh in the university library and nothing of worth online. The closest I got was a bio of some secondary-school teacher from north Meath who had the same initials and surname. There was even less on Camland. And now that I thought about it, the idea of a sasquatch sighting in north Kildare was as cracked as it got.

The movie came to an end and I quickly turned off the television. I unhooked Maebh's HDMI cord. I shut down her laptop.

And, as expected, I dreamed of gourds.

In the morning it was clear I had to see Simone.

Over Nesquik, Maebh joked about gourds. I deflected as best I could. It was possible she was pranking me, she had done such things before. Like putting mayonnaise in my piña colada, mailing me love letters from my crushes. This scenario was a little different. But I didn't put it past her.

My reasoning was that either she was lying and she was in on it, or she was telling the truth and I was fucked.

So at 9 a.m. I hightailed it to Simone's office. I paused at her door, where I saw that her office hours were between 2 and 4 p.m. But this couldn't wait. It was an emergency, I *had* to see her. What was more, I knew she was in there. I could hear her typing away, smacking the keys of her laptop as though playing whack-a-mole.

I knocked.

'Come in!'

I opened the door and started unloading immediately.

'I'm *so* sorry, Simone, really sorry, believe me. I know it's not your office hours and I get that, but it's an emergency? I don't want to be another casualty, another Laird, another—'

The weighted door slammed shut, startling us both. I looked into Simone's perturbed, Dodger Blue eyes.

'Can I sit down?'

'Of course.'

Then her fastidiousness got the better of her and she corrected my grammar.

'You *may*.'

The ensuing days were horrendous.

It was bad enough that Simone refuted virtually everything I said; bad enough she did so in a friendly and flippant way, the way one pal might say to another, 'Cedric, you'd make a *terrible* carpenter. Don't pursue the matter any further and become a midwife instead.' But other calamities occurred too. Maebh, for example, was overly sympathetic. She could see I was stressed, by a terrible breakout I was having, the kind whose volcanic cysts spurt for twenty minutes after they pop. So she bought me a tea-tree oil exfoliator to combat my bodily reaction to worry. But I saw through her shtick: she was just trying to cover up the fact that she was gaslighting me.

Then there were my parents, who were also giving me grief. Texts, voicemails, the lot. They didn't understand why I wouldn't come home for Christmas, why I hadn't been home since I left for Maynooth in September. It was simple: they hated me. And why would I go somewhere I was hated?

It had been Maebh's idea to stay in Maynooth for Christmas. And though I was unsure whether I could trust her anymore, I was looking forward to it. We planned to have fillet steaks and martinis.

But the worst thing about those horrendous few days was that, two days after I dropped into Simone's office, I was fired from Humble Steve's.

Indeed.

A beach ball of a man rolled up to my stand in a red Lacrosse polo so big it'd have covered a Hummer. He wore wrap-around shades on the indigo side of blue; black jeans, too long, accordingly frayed at the edges; and two-strap sandals with an argyle pair of socks. Holding his hand was his matchstick of a daughter, who wore a unicorn onesie, hood up, horn pointing at me. They deliberated over my ice creams for what felt like two hours.

All was chill until I handed the girl a mint-chocolate cone. (I know – who takes *two hours* to decide on mint-fucking-chocolate?) Then it became clear that my services didn't meet her standards.

'The *sprinkles*! You forgot the *sprinkles*!' she said.

Well that did it. I yanked the cone from her hands and threw it so far away that I didn't hear it when it dropped. But I saw it land at the opposite end of the shopping centre, by the gammy-legged trolleys, in a mushroom cloud of ice cream. Most people were shocked. But I think one guy applauded: an incel coming out of Game with a fresh bag of swag.

Then the Beach Ball and I argued and deftly exchanged obscenities until his voice dropped to a whisper and, through clenched teeth, he told me:

'Kelly here has non-Hodgkin's.'

And at that I wanted to stick my head in the nearest bucket of ice cream.

'Ah balls, I'm really sorry,' I said.

'The wigs are itchy on her head. Which is why she loves her onesie. Don't you, hon?'

She nodded. She was smiling. There were specks of orange in her eyes, which otherwise were hazel. Her father, I think, was crying.

I quickly made another ice cream and doused the thing in sprinkles and apologised again. Then to make further amends I gave them the whole bucket of mint-chocolate.

'That, ah … that really won't be necessary,' the Beach Ball said.

'No no, I insist.' I slapped the lid on the bucket. To seal the deal. 'Sorry again. Been a crazy few days.'

The Beach Ball slowly took the tub and Kelly waved at me as they left.

It was a successful resolution. Or so I thought.

Humble Steve believed otherwise. He appeared an hour later to relieve me of my shift. When I told him the truth about how I had successfully defused a PR nightmare for him and his blossoming company, he fired me on the spot while pointing at the exit.

'Walk out that door and don't stop until you hit the West. Then swim into the Atlantic and don't stop until you drown.'

'Jesus, Steve. A bit extreme, no?'

He didn't say anything. He averted his eyes and scowled into the bucket of raspberry cookie dough.

'One last ice cream before I go?' I said.

'Get out!'

So I left.

For sure: a bad time. Out of work, out of luck. But I was working mainly for pint money. I had saved enough the previous summer to cover my rent for the year. I'd need a job after Christmas, but that was a problem to solve later on. For now, Maebh and Simone both said that what I *claimed* transpired in the Iontas basement was something for which I should seek professional help. So mulling over that took up most of my time until Christmas.

But somehow I knew they were gaslighting me. They had to be, there was no other explanation. I didn't tell them this, however. I thanked them for their concern. I put my head down and I thought. I went back to the source of the problem three days after I was fired: I went back to the Iontas basement. But to my surprise the doors were locked. And they remained locked every day, until eventually I stopped checking.

And yet I had leads.

Two of them. To be precise.

The first was that *Dwelobnik* was real. Simone confirmed as much in her office, when we talked about 'my worries'. Along with a little about Laird's disappearance. And *Dwelobnik*. She said that Olivia O'Shaughnessy was an old college pal of hers and had indeed secured funding for a new literary magazine earlier in the year. She was surprised I hadn't heard about it. There had been an announcement over the summer, while the first submission window opened in September.

'You really didn't know?' she said, as if testing me.

'No.'

'Hm. Strange.'

Either way, the magazine was real and I learned of it in the basement, through Simone.

The second lead I had was Cian Scanlon, my final card to play. But I wasn't keen to contact him since he was the last person on whom my sanity depended. And if he also denied the existence of the Cucurbitaceae Club and Camland, I was fucked.

Because the stakes were so high, then, I put it off for a while.

At the time I didn't give a shit about Camland. I was curious, but there was no professional imperative for me to pursue the thing any further. After my meeting in Gourd City, the only thing I wanted to verify was that I wasn't crazy. Everything else – my actual interest in Camland and my idea for the three-dimensional narrative – came later.

I demurred. I focused on my essays and my upcoming Christmas exams. I told the family once more that I wasn't coming home. But it was trickier now, since Maebh had caved. Two weeks into December she told me of her decision to return to Sligo for Christmas.

'And what am I supposed to do? Grill asparagus for one?' I said.

'Go *home*. Your parents *miss* you.'

'They do, yeah.'

I wasn't budging.

And I told my mother as much on the phone one night.

'Why?' I said.

I was in bed, on my second bottle of wine, a cheap Aldi red. Maebh was gone at this stage.

'Why what?' my mother said.

'Why would I come home to a family that hates me?'

'How is this still going on, Darren? Nothing happened last summer like you said it did. I was so glad to have you around. In the hospital and at home. Your board game was adorable. It *is* adorable. I love it. Why wouldn't it have cheered me up? We can play it when you're home?'

Then I reached out for more wine and spilled it onto Maebh's mattress.

'Fuck. I'll call you back.'

I hung up and didn't call back.

*

My father practically had to drag me out of the flat.

He drove up in his Mercedes the afternoon of Christmas Adam and banged on the door until the Turkish barbers popped their heads out. (They both worked and lived below us.) He flew up the stairs and invited himself in. I took a good look at him and suppressed a laugh.

He had grown a real lawn of a chin-strap. A smig. It was revolting. And *brown*.

For all my life, my father's had a vicious head of black curls. Legend has it that his hair once broke a Cork barber's shears. It's never receded. Nor has its sheen ever decreased in brilliance, which leads me to believe that he dyes it in secret.

The hue of his smig therefore gave his face a new depth. It drew out the quiet fury in his eyes, it lent his jaw a new poetry.

And he said that if I didn't go home it would kill my poor mother.

And that, I regret to say, did it.

I imagined my mother in her coffin as I lay coasters at her wake, so that relatives and family friends and parishioners and colleagues didn't stain our table, our mantelpiece, our floor, not with their cups of instant coffee and their lukewarm, metallic tea, or their bottles of lagers, their Millers and Molsons and Budweisers. I imagined laying her favourite coasters, the sailboat ones we got in Portugal when Nick, being seven, frolicked in the sea and I, being fourteen, ogled every pair of tits I could see. I imagined distributing these coasters, then looking at my mother's oak casket and seeing her hands jasmine-white with death. I imagined tearing up, violently and without warning, as I realised I would never talk to her again.

So I relented and I cried and I told my father I'd go home.

And in the car we listened to Radio Nova until we drove beyond its bandwidth. My father turned the volume up to stifle my quiet sobbing. The channel cut out around Enfield, just before the guitar solo at the end of 'Hotel California', after which Ger fiddled with the radio wheel by his indicator. Between blasts of white noise we caught a snippet of Shakin' Stevens or Wizard on Christmas FM. Then he hit pre-set four and KFM was playing country, the old and lonesome shit, and I was grateful the music had nothing to do with Christmas.

'You're all right, boss,' my dad said, slapping my knee.

But I didn't think I was.

Christmas, however, was lovely. So lovely, in fact, I'd rather not talk about it. Like Laird, it's too sad in retrospect.

But because Christmas was a hoot, I was more optimistic when I returned to Tiny Palace in January. Even Maebh said I was perkier. I got a new job, bartending part-time in Tallon's. I lied on my CV and said I had worked in my uncle's pub in Tipperary the previous summer. The reference number was Maebh's. But John Tallon never rang her. He offered me the job in the interview and I started the next day.

As for Scanlon, I remained unsure. In the new year I was certainly less edgy than I was in December, so I considered not hitting him up at all. I wondered if it might be better to cut my losses, to forget about Gourd City entirely.

And I almost did.

But when February came around and I learned I did terribly in my exams – nothing but 2:1s – I had little choice.

Within two days of my results I scheduled an appointment for the Writing Centre.

5

They came with much controversy, the beginnings of said Writing Centre. Not because they grew out of that garish feat of architectural monstrosity, the North Campus's Arts Block, but because of some bureaucratic hullabaloo that involved sub-minimum wage pay when the centre was established. Soon it became a part of general Maynooth lore: everyone had heard of it but few could tell you what it was about.

'Stingy bastards,' certain students would say, passing the doors of the centre, though they were uncertain of whom they were blaspheming and for what exact reason. Many were merely waiting to get into TH1 for another lecture in which they would try hard to make notes on *The Playboy of the Western World* but harder still to stay awake in the theatre's blistering heat. (There were very few rooms at Maynooth that accorded an agreeable temperature.)

Since it was custom for Scanlon to meet with first-time users before assigning them a tutor, my debut appearance at the centre was to be no different. I asked the History minors in my class what he was like. More than one said he was a hot-headed nutjob. Curious, I sat in on a lecture of his to confirm. It was poorly attended, I didn't see a single woman, but my peers were correct. Scanlon's aura was deranged. The zealous eyes, the formal diction, the Derry accent, the Hellenic curls, his use of the indefinite article *an* in conjunction with the qualifier *historical*. For everyone in this room, I imagined, these characteristics marked their first encounter with the gravity of academia. They saw in Scanlon that his profession was neither a job nor a game but a battle in which the stakes were costly. Of course they didn't share the same opinion. To them college was just a means by which to collect the grant, to get the ride, to have the craic. But on Scanlon's jowl-winged face they detected an earnest approach to mental labour they'd take pains in their lives never to replicate. They were dossers, bollixes, lads. They weren't cut out for that sort of thing.

This performative persona of Scanlon's rarely left the lecture hall. In person, I learned, he was placid and meek, receptive and kind. He carried about him at all times a bottle of Nestlé Iced Tea and, funnily for an academic, always wore jeans, never a suit. In his blue eyes danced the youthfulness of a lifelong bachelor. His demeanour was blemished by loneliness, and seemed to epitomise that of the cautious man who had graciously accepted a life of virtual celibacy. To look at him was to admit he appeared far younger than fifty-two.

Our first meeting was insightful, efficacious. I took something of a beating but emerged a more attentive writer. Scanlon adopted a clinical approach to the craft of prose, wherein he eliminated every second word to better focus on why your writing was shit. And after analysing a sample of mine he could pinpoint where I was going wrong: dangling modifiers, faulty parallelisms, obscure arguments, arcane vocabulary. He advised me to borrow some writing manuals from the library – *Elements of Style*, *Tools for the Craft*, *The Reader over Your Shoulder* – and to take out back, shoot, burn and bury every thesaurus I had ever owned.

I complied forthwith and subsequently met with Kate, an MA student of Irish Studies from whom I regularly scrounged a smoke, enjoying, in the process, a conversation about the superiority of Drum tobacco over Amber Leaf.

And not long after that, Camland besieged my blood.

To iterate, I consulted Cian Scanlon not to seek out Camland but to ensure I wouldn't graduate with a 2:1. Young though I was, I realised there were few jobs in the world for which I was adequately suited. I began to worry about this. My thinking was that if eventually I was to assume a life of permanent precarity, I wanted at least a first-class degree as my starry sky at which to stare from the gutter.

Thus I found myself obsessing about academia more generally. It was the only thing I cared about. I dreamed of tenure by the water. At NUI Galway or the University of Sussex. I was no longer the financial wreck I was a year-and-a-bit ago. But I craved a literary discovery that I wasn't getting from the modernist novella or British literature of the 1930s. Sure, when I was slinging pints, I was thinking about Aschenbach, Dalloway, Gregor, Kurtz, Gatsby; and when I listened to lectures, I was transcribing words in my head, absorbing the wisdom of faculty in order to utilise it for exam purposes. But on the occasions I rang home, I zoned out at my mother's mention of Viennese fingers or her current state of being and I thought of what I'd write for my doctorate, my post-doc, my future articles, my monographs.

Then around mid-March it clicked.

I realised there was little new to say in the overcrowded world of academia. It was not so much a cut-throat business as an adult-sized playground in which the rules were 'Finders keepers' and 'My da's bigger than yours'; in which the father, of course, was an outlandish reading of a literary work. Critics fought over the first word, then over who said it better. And what was Camland, I wondered, if not a subject about which I was guaranteed the first word? What was it if not, all going well, an academic goldmine? Or gourdmine, if you please.

Further thoughts came immediately. The first PhD candidate in Camish Studies. Doctoral funding, sponsored post-docs, tenure, a stable life. An eminent career. What Richard Ellmann was to James Joyce, or Judith Butler to Gender Studies, Darren Walton would be to all things Camish.

So one afternoon I shot Cian Scanlon an email.

'Dear Cian,' it went. 'I do not believe I have reached out to you yet since I availed of your staff's exceptional services. I am more confident with my writing than ever before, and for that I have you to thank. Know that it is very much appreciated. In addition, I am thinking about researching the topic of Camland. Professor Longford of the English department first ran it past me a few months ago and said that you may know a thing or two about it. If this is something with which you would be interested in assisting me, do let me know. Best, Darren.'

As the above makes clear, in the space of six writing consultations I had become outrageously dull, muddled by cliché, hackneyed by exposition. All in a quest for clarity and precision.

My idealism had reached a point where the basis for my career was now an obscure topic about which I knew nothing and whose peculiar existence was too *new* to have any discernible relation to truth. After all, in the academy, the more veracious the argument, the older the essay. But that was precisely what fascinated me about Camland. It was, as I imagined – before I knew a single thing about it – novelty masked as truth. Which is exactly what the academy were after.

Those precious stones that lie at the heart of an exquisite poem? They've been on sale for centuries, have done the rounds to such a promiscuous extent that they're practically worthless. No faculty wants them. They hate your diamonds, spurn your emeralds, loathe your topazes, spit on your opals, piss on your rubies, laugh in the face of your turquoises and sapphires. They want dirt disguised as hydrophanes, mulch passed off as aquamarine. Or if you can pull the feat off, water in the form of cymophanes or chrysoberyls.

(Apologies for including such obscure jewels. Years ago I was haunted by Maebh's brooch to such an extent that I tried to find it online, and though I failed to do so, I fell down a jewel-themed rabbit hole during which I committed the above gems to memory.)

Standing, then, before what I thought was a genuine break with the past, before the future of Ireland, I imagined I had found the perfect way to conflate novelty and truth. All without burning out. From my essays it was clear that I had nothing to say and I insisted on saying it. That I was less an advocate of noble silence than a practitioner of dishonourable clamour. That I relished the noise where meaning and nothingness rhymed. But with Scanlon's project I suspected I might have a lifeline. A means by which to say nothing and, in doing so, attain a career.

If, that is, my hunch was correct.

Scanlon replied the following day. The email's timestamp was 03:32 of that morning.

I would remember this timestamp years later, when the email thread disappeared. How wouldn't I? The man was replying to me in the early hours of a Tuesday morning. I've no doubt they were real, these emails, but where did they go? Do they live on a server in some north Dublin suburb? Did a Microsoft employee permanently erase them from Outlook? Did Scanlon or Simone have a role to play in their disappearance? Was my computer bugged, even at this early stage?

I don't know. But what Scanlon said was this.

'Hi Darren, Many thanks for the kind words. I'm delighted you benefitted from our services. As for Camland, your interest is thrilling. Given the complexity of the topic, however, it might be best if we have a wee chat in person. My office hours are 11:00–13:00 on Tuesdays and 15:00–17:00 on Wednesdays. But if these don't suit, we can schedule a time that works for us both. Yours, Cian.'

I met him the following day and received a crash course in Camland. Everything started in 2004 at an inter-disciplinary convention at University College Dublin, for the dissemination of alternative histories. There Scanlon conceived the idea for Camland while listening to Sophie Confey, a Mathematics professor at St John's College, Cambridge, deliver a paper about a subject whose specifics I can't remember. At the sandwich table following Sophie's paper, he proposed it to others and was tastefully shot down by more than one person.

The biggest issue his interlocutors had was that his proposal impinged upon the present day. It was no doubt compelling, it could make for a good paper, but were there a book on the matter, they said, it would take conspiracy or yellow journalism as its primary methodology. And even in the cloisters of alternative history, that was a big problem.

Nonetheless, word spread. At the end of the convention academics from across the country were approaching him. From Dublin City University, University College Cork, Trinity College Dublin, NUI Galway, the University of Limerick, the University of Ulster. Even some from abroad wanted to participate in Camland's construction. Scanlon was grateful, overwhelmed at the response, but was so new to the idea himself that he didn't know where to begin. He was a film producer, if you will, with only a meagre logline for a three-hour epic. Now the onus was on him to assemble a coherent script and a justifiable shooting schedule.

To this end, he and his participants created a website whose garish design was cutting edge for its time, and on it they sketched out key events in Camish history. The underground publication of Syngechair Loolah's *Notes Towards a Theory of Camish Culture* in August 1924; the Cookstown Address of 1936; the assassination of Whitefin McGettrick, first Taoiseach of Camland, by the reprobate Betty Gazpacho on January 2, 1953. These events built up to their collective signing of the Proclamation of the Camish Republic in 2005. The articles comprising the website Scanlon had on file, but no library or internet database would ever possess them. The website, moreover, was long since defunct.

By early 2008 he came into luck when he procured for his team a book deal with Bloomsbury Academic. In late 2009, however, while he was line editing *Freedom and Fish Ovens: An Introduction to Camland*, representatives at Cambridge University Press contacted Bloomsbury with a cease and desist. They were not, they said, in a position to disclose why Scanlon's project needed to stop. But they insisted that if Scanlon or anyone else dared commit another sentence to their master Word document, the careers of all those involved would come to a precipitate and premature end.

The letter produced the desired effect. Scanlon deleted the Word doc and told everyone to adopt a new hobby horse. He was especially disappointed about the timing, because only the day before he had roped in three members from Maynooth's Physics department to further assist the project. There were many similarities between alternative histories, quantum mechanics, string theory and physical cosmology.

He told me as much.

*

'It's right simple,' he said, during that first office meeting. The lilt of his accent periodically rose, sporadically fell. He spoke slowly. Carefully.

'When you enter the workforce in earnest, Darren? You'll quickly realise that the higher up you go, the less work you'll do. But with Camland? That's simply not the case. I started this project, this little ditty of a pastime? As something of a joke or a means to keep going.'

His hazardous workspace, in which there was almost no room to sit for the columns of books and piles of paper around us, offered distractions aplenty. Atop his bookcases were an unhealthy number of VHSs for a room in the early 2010s. He had a beige assortment of fresher Film-major faves: Lynch, Coppola, Scorsese, Tarantino, Haneke, Kubrick; no one with a uterus.

'I'm only saying that as I pursued this particular line of thought? I was silenced by Cambridge, and the higher I climbed, the *more* work I'd to do. It got to the point where I was afraid? To conduct research online? In case Cambridge could trace me. About four years ago now. And nothing's budged since.'

He pronounced nothing like nottin, a linguistic tic I've always loved in a Derryman.

'Those who were on board with the idea in the beginning? They've long fled, Darren. I'm on me own, so I am.'

Leaning into a drawer he pulled out a thick Manila folder. He tossed it onto his desk. Some papers spooled out. The force with which it smacked the wood was jarring. I was no longer myself. Instead I was a detective from the potboilers of my youth, a figure from a plot by Harlan Coben, Michael Connelly, Patricia Cornwell, John Grisham. For a moment I believed I was a character, a nobody, not so much a conduit for a real person, your best friend, your parents, your ex, your boss as a waste of space, a recipient of prayers, a scream down the road that you may or may not have heard, the call of a loon, the gulp of a madman drowning, a patient breathing her last in abject isolation.

For a moment, indeed, I *was* nobody, and in this space I felt relieved. Here there was no anger, no fear, sex, destruction, no friendship or dyads, no split, no you-go-here-and-I-*thall-ansin*, no signs in which the English o'er Irish chimed and the tourists stopped to laugh at *leithris*, no forking paths and choices stark but one toppling layered simulation wherein all choices played themselves out fully and through them a certain truth emerged and verily clung one's life to this.

My thoughts, it was clear, were doing backflips. They congregated in the hinterland while my desires were on the waterfront. They were simultaneously complementing and conspiring against my desires.

I wanted in as much as out, to fight as much as flee.

But I also wanted Scanlon to tell me more. For I was seduced by his fictions, by the simulation of constructed lies. My suspicion was that Camland offered a better way of looking at the world than any critical theory could offer. That it would yield better tastes and sensations than Simone Longford's gourds.

But I was frightened of its stature. Here to me was fiction as it was, as it should be, truly bouncing off and not reflecting society, history, commerce. It was charged, dangerous, messy, volatile, sweaty, taut, grim. The mere presence of the folder had increased the voltage of the room, and Scanlon's diction was doing its best to transmogrify the uncanny and whoosh it in my general direction.

'This folder, in essence, is all I can think about,' he said. 'They're copies? So take your time with her? No need to be bringing them back before you've turned them over? You'll know then when you're done if it's more research you want to be doing. Don't rush her?'

He turned and looked out the window and in his reflection I detected the cold glaze of insecure thoughts. A yearning for a more uninformed time. His degree of earnestness was so overbaked that I began to doubt the sincerity of his speech. Given the depths he stooped to convey his solemnity, you'd swear he was after giving me ten sheets of acid.

'This isn't about the underdog or … *sticking it to the man*, as the telly says. S'not about … the master–slave dialectic? There *is* no underdog here, no political unconscious. This is about freedom? The liberty to revise and reinvent and change the way we think? When people discover things, Darren, it's not so much the object of discovery that fascinates them. No. What's fascinating, I tell you, is the object's thing-in-itself. Or the fact it's undiscovered? And that's why, until the object enters the larger world and assumes a new life for itself, the discoverers take so much pleasure in exclaiming that nobody knows about it. "It's here?" they say. "We have it. And nobody knows about it." More common than you think. Hipsters who uncover a hot new band? Literary critics on a neglected classic? Historians discussing momentous events that evaded public knowledge until now? *Nobody knows about it.* It's the eternal refrain, so it is.'

He finally looked away from the window and back at me.

If there was one thing his speech suggested, it was that he was batshit as much as brilliant, and I couldn't yet tell whether this was a lethal or a harmless combination.

'When you have that kind of information?' he frowned, shaking his head. 'You're not an underdog. You're not a bum? You're at the top of the hierarchy, you're a king. Some see you as God? And that's why Cambridge, that's why they won't stop me from pursuing this matter. They can try? Can slow me down. But they can't take away my ability to research. There's something in Camland. And although I can't say for sure what in God's name that is, I know it's enough to keep going. I could give you the drivel. Camland's about freedom, Camland's about envisioning Ireland as she never was in order to understand her as she is now. But what good would that be? Dive into those papers yonder and tell me that's all there is to it? I daresay you can't.'

He shoved the folder off the table. It fell neatly into my lap. Then he tilted his head doorwise as if I were cattle. *Gwan, git*, he might well have said, slapping my arse and clapping me forward. It would have been no more befuddling than the words he had just spouted.

I nodded in thanks and got to my feet. I lumbered clumsily out of Rhetoric House. I knew my dossier full of papers might be more at home in a skip, but I also knew there was no chance of my binning them.

And on the walk back to Tiny Palace I kept hearing echoes.

Of Scanlon's sedate, eldritch speech.

6

Back at Tiny Palace, Maebh was stewing beef. She didn't ask about the folder, which I thought somewhat suspicious. We exchanged a few howyas and yeah-not-a-bothers; our preferred prelude to an evening of doing our own things, keeping ourselves to our headphones until, if neither of us was going out, sitting down over hot whiskeys and Jammie Dodgers to watch the nine o'clock news. Followed by, when we were really sucking diesel, an episode of *Prime Time Investigates*. But that evening I holed myself up at the kitchenette table in order to make headway on the Land of Calm.

Now that I had cooled down after meeting Scanlon, I could form my own opinion about the world he'd been building when

Cambridge suppressed his project, and it didn't take long to see that he and his retinue of scholars were invested in the study of a vast, fictitious social formation.

In the folder were curious things. Elaborate sketches of Camish beaches and forestry. A timeline of the necktie in the history of Camland. Over a hundred snippets of conversation from Camish pubgoers since 1962. A series of newspaper articles for *The Darglar Dispatch*, in which it was repeated that Krickles O'Shea, inventor of the Pikerowave, would soon appear in court on charges of tax evasion. But among them too were more scientific curios: a jittery synopsis of John Everett's many-worlds interpretation of the universe; a Socratic dialogue wherein quantum physicists discussed 'bulks' in a higher dimension colliding with another 'membrane' and thereby causing a Big Bang; meticulous drawings of the six 'regular convex 4-polytopes', about which I hitherto hadn't a clue but which I feared would bring on a migraine if I looked at them for too long, especially the final sketch in the series, whose psychedelic intricacy made me question what I was letting myself in for, since physics and mathematics didn't usually lie within the jurisdiction of my knowledge.

This was a world of state-sanctioned, virtual-reality headsets, a world of preposterous names. Billcifers, Páifreachs and Dr Soups coincided alongside the likes of Pernerloppy Flynns and Laura Huyanos. The farce of one continually trumped the other. While it was no utopia – Camland was very clearly Ireland in drag, replete with its flaws and shortcomings, its strengths and kinks – it displayed an equal tendency towards the fantastical as the absurd. Here was a place in which anthropomorphic pencils contended with disease, in which hermaphrodite oracles prophesised at microwave-themed amusement parks, in which the staff at a St Jonathan's Hospital were required *by law* to wear clown costumes on the job. (The primary treatment at this hospital were readings from the work of Lippen D. Verzgort, an obscure Dutch philosopher whose aphorisms eradicated more cancers, doctors said, than chemotherapy and surgery combined.) Every town had a new name and the counties were no different. The island of Ireland now looked something like this:

As I thought more critically about the dossier's contents, the project's purpose remained elusive. If it was world-building Scanlon was after, he should have written a novel, not a work of spurious non-fiction. I started to suspect alternative histories wasn't a credible area of historical studies and, worse, that Camland might not present me an opportunity to clinch academic fame.

Were these contributors real? Was *I* real? Did I need another drink? I did. So I opened a bottle of wine.

Then a quick Google search further aroused my suspicions. According to the internet, there had never been a convention for alternative histories at UCD, let alone in 2004. (I was aware, however, that the absence of something online didn't necessitate its non-existence.) Likewise disquieting were the module guides of history programs across the country, for none contained the phrase 'alternative histories'. Not even the descriptor for Maynooth's Historiography III, which Cian Scanlon taught.

More reassuring was that the academics whose names appeared throughout the folder were genuine. For the most part. There were only two whose existence I couldn't ascertain: Louise Davies and Adrian Killam. All of which brought me to three possible conclusions.

I tested them out on Maebh.

'Ms Kealy?' I said to our bedroom wall.

She scurried from the bedroom.

'Mr Walton?'

'Let's have a shot.'

So we did. A Jäger each. Then I made us both tea. I was anxious to tell her of my conclusions. But when she pointed to the mess on the table and asked, with a pursed lip, what the fuck it was all about, I summarised the contents and took my time. Maebh rolled a joint, then moved to the window to smoke it. This pleased me, because she was always more engaged when she was high.

By the time I got to my conclusions my speech had increased in speed.

'The first possibility is that the contents were written exclusively by Scanlon. But this results in two conflicting corollaries: either the alleged contributors are aware of the project and they vetoed the ghost-written pieces, or they're unaware of Scanlon's fraudulent behaviour and the essays are an act of identity theft.'

'Sunshine, *slow down.*'

Maebh rolled the roach between her fingers.

I ignored her plea.

'The second conclusion is that the project *is* collaborative and the two questionable contributors were PhD candidates who failed to complete their degrees or secure post-doctoral fellowships. Or, they decided they wanted out of academia post-PhD. That the folder contains no biographies for the contributors also enhances the likelihood of this theory.'

'Can you *please* stop talking like you're reading an essay?'

'I'm almost done. The final conclusion is that the project is in fact collaborative, but the contributors, in going with the nature of their methodology, decided to invent two fake contributors. Why they would do this for anything other than gits and shiggles, however, is hard to grasp.'

'I think—'

'Bottom line: either alternative histories is entirely in Scanlon's head and everything he told me about Cambridge's intervention was a lie, or alternative history is a secret methodology among Irish historians, and potentially physicists too, and Cambridge are keen to shut him down. But if so, why? What could Cambridge have on the project that Scanlon doesn't?'

There was a pause during which the warbling of birds flitted in through the window. Then Maebh said:

'Or, it's entirely in *your* head.'

She opened the undersink cupboard and binned her roach in the compost. I felt as I did in the Iontas basement.

Alone.

'You're just stoned,' I said, trying to let on that her words didn't worry me.

'And *you're* drunk. But look – that's *your* handwriting right there.'

She moved to the table and circled my marginalia with a finger. I saw she had a hangnail, which I instantly wanted to rip off.

'Those are just notes.'

'Okay, sunshine. If you say so.'

She was fucking with me.

Surely?

In that moment she was less a friend than a purveyor of paranoia from whom I wished to run away.

So I did.

'I'm going for a walk,' I said.

Maebh nodded and went for the bedroom. She poked me in the stomach as she passed.

'Let me know if you come across any anthropomorphic pencils on your travels.'

When I got back, Maebh was asleep. The dossier was still on the table. I sat down and reassessed my thoughts.

Fraud, secrecy, solipsism, fiction, physics, the academy. The signifiers didn't cohere.

I continued reading the dossier.

Quickly I understood the temptation of fraud. With academics to its name like Ailbhe Marlborough (UCC) and Luke Oppenheimer (University of York) and Sophie Confey (St John's, Cambridge),

Scanlon's finished book would be an accomplishment. No wonder Bloomsbury were once on board. But the question of conspiracy was opaque at best. While there was a clandestine touch to the dossier, it lacked the urgency that most secrets radiate. Its tone was at odds with its content; the former promised riches while the latter suggested coppers. The layered narrative was compelling only because it implied a pay-off. Scanlon *et al.* implied throughout the papers that the discourse of Camland would be to the twenty-first century what those of Freud, Lacan, Adorno, Saussure, Derrida, Foucault, Butler, Lyotard, Blanchot, Sontag, Kristeva and others were to the twentieth. But not once did they make good on this promise.

And by the dossier's midpoint, Camland had my interest but nothing more, as I began to wonder if it was a fruitless pursuit. The more I ruminated, the more obscure things became. I couldn't tell if I was becoming stumped or enlightened. There was Blue Turnip, the nineteenth-century evolutionary biologist who penned *Crop Rotation Couples* (1865); Dietrich Kavanagh, medieval king of Fairytop whose castle was strewn with pieces of amusing trivia; a young girl from Slopium who for all her life wanted to be a gromtomite – whatever that was – but never succeeded in bringing her dreams to fruition. I suspected that Scanlon had ties to Opus Dei or the Masons – or the Cucurbitaceae Club – and was keeping silent about it. But these were just fleeting theories, of which there would come to be many.

Then at 4 a.m. I came across a green Post-it note, stuck to the last paper-clipped bundle I had yet to read. On it were hefty blue blocks: 'THE POINT OF CAMLAND IS TO CONSIDER ALTERNATIVES. MY CAMISH NIECE HARRIET FARRELL GETS THIS. WITH HER ON BOARD EVERYTHING CLICKS.'

I debated. Bed or tea? Read further or no? Abandon, commit?

I deliberated over the matter while eating two Jammie Dodgers over the kitchen sink.

Then I made tea and pawed another two Dodgers and I finished the dossier.

The little I found out about Harriet Farrell, I regret to say, did light something of a conflagration under my feet. But not for the reasons you might suspect.

Scanlon made it clear throughout his last notes that to trace Harriet's genealogy was to trace that of Camland itself. And that the result clarified the Ireland–Camland binary. As Scanlon wrote himself, 'to understand Harriet Farrell and Camland, one must consider Harriet's genealogy and how she sees herself within it, and how her lineage slots within the duality of Camland and Ireland. After which the rest is noise. For the point of Camland is simply to tell a story.'

If Camland, then, existed solely to reinforce the idea of history as narrative, history as this totalising system in which to elucidate the past, the evident argument of Scanlon's project was that narrative, not cash, rules everything around us. Which was a bland enough statement. Almost as bland as his final piece, whose static content and banal delivery was at odds with everything I had read so far. It was simply a piece of family history in which Scanlon wrote of the Farrells' gradual move from the Candle (Wicklow) Mountains to the leafy environs of Mawko (Dalkey), with particular time devoted to the family's ideological shift from Doggaholism (Catholicism) to that of the Church of Camland.

And for all I wondered whether Scanlon was the genuine author, at this stage it didn't matter. Given the bathetic flop of the dossier's conclusion, I knew I would never wrangle a career out of Camland.

I knew there was no point in taking my Camish Thoughts further.

But it wasn't that simple.

For while I was reading and stewing over the Farrells, I caught a first glimpse of Camland as a stepping stone to an idea that *was* my own.

The three-dimensional narrative.

*

The genesis of my complex narrative theory was organic if causal: I reacted to Scanlon's prose with sensible questions and no-nonsense analysis and, in the end, what I arrived at was the beginnings of my theory.

It happened like so.

If Harriet was meant to be a kind of Camish Everywoman, she was criminally underdeveloped. If she was meant to represent a specific person in Irish history, the synecdoche was lost on me. The females in Scanlon's essay were entirely subordinated to men, and the males who dominated the narrative were more stale than a punctured packet of crisps. Then there was the question of surnames. Those of the Farrells were not untoward, as were those of everyone else I had read about in the dossier. It was as if Scanlon had transcribed the real-life history of an Irish family and had forgot to change their surname to suit the whims of Camish people. Moreover, what Scanlon had was a snapshot of family history. Unless he planned to do more with it, it was useless.

All of which complicated Scanlon's purpose for the project. If Camland's point was to consider, if not expose, alternatives, to whom was Harriet Farrell an alternative? If Camland's point was to tell a story, why was Harriet's tale limited not so much to its first act as to the first minutes of its opening (and excruciatingly boring) scenes? If Scanlon believed in the totality of history and how it rules our lives for the better, where was the totality of Harriet's history? What was its significance? After all, it was through Harriet, allegedly, that everything clicked into place.

As I swept biscuit crumbs into my lap, I saw that Camland was a one-dimensional construct. A straight line between two fixed coordinates, whose magnificent structure would never reveal itself to me. Primarily because *it was not there*. Because it didn't exist. Camland, I felt, was a story in which no character had an arc, in which there were no second or third acts. Camland was a story without themes. And what's a theme if it doesn't develop? What's a story if it doesn't unfold but rather remains static for an unspecified time, contracts measles, then dies? What's a plot point if it appears for a page, only to disappear and never be seen again? What's a character if she neither acts nor thinks?

While my mind ran amok in response to these questions, my stomach lurched. For I knew I could never turn Scanlon's nebulous ideas into a decent proposal, let alone an 80,000-word thesis on which to secure a career. I realised that if I still wanted to be an academic, I would have to direct my critical energies elsewhere.

But *where*?

To plunge deeper into the project would be a mistake. That was clear. The only thing Scanlon could offer me was an elaborate means by which to squander my time. His ideas made sense on the surface, but ultimately they masked a reality with no substance. Or a substance to whose secrets I would never be privy.

In short, Scanlon's dots didn't line up.

It really was as if he had given me acid.

It was then I noticed the shifting dots on the pages, the undulating lines and bulges, as though a physical matter were trying to break free from the paper. Immediately I knew what was happening. I was tripping. But I hadn't partaken of any psychedelic substances, I had only consumed a soupçon of booze, so how the fuck was this happening? Maebh couldn't have spiked me. Unless she had spiked the Jammie Dodgers. Which I doubted. She went to bed at 9 and it was now 6 a.m. So that didn't add up either.

But, rolling with it, I studied the shapes and quickly flicked back to the polytopes. On account of my visual shifting, their geometric symmetry was enchanting. So much so that I was no longer angry or disappointed with the dossier.

I reconsidered Scanlon's argument and pushed my lap-crumbs to the floor.

If narrative, as Scanlon implied, was a panopticon whose detection we can never evade, did it work the other way? Was it a continuum of sorts? Scanlon suggested that in the hands of the wrong author, narrative was more oppressive than a gulag. But with the right author at the helm, might it be more liberating than an acquittal?

I wasn't entirely sure of what I was trying to say. But I remembered an earlier section of the dossier, John Everett's many-worlds interpretation of the universe, and what little I understood of it.

'There is always more than one narrative,' I said to the empty kitchenette.

Then I looked back to the polytopes, which were no longer shifting. They reminded me that good narratives were never one-dimensional. I pushed the dossier aside, resolved to go no further with Camland. It was an equation so complex that no human could derive it. Only a god, I thought, his machine rusty in descent, could save us from its convolutions.

And yet, I wondered.

If Camland was a one-dimensional narrative and a good yarn was two-dimensional, what would it mean if a narrative was three- or four-dimensional? What if narratives had coordinates not just on the x-axis, nor on the x and the y-axis, but on the x and the y *and* the z-axis? What if a narrative had an infinite amount of variables or permutations? What might the axes stand for? What if they never ended?

I grabbed a loose sheet of dossier-paper and started plotting coordinates.

I no longer felt like I was tripping.

In fact, I had never felt more sober in all my life.

Step Two

Alt-Dwelobnik

Z = NaN

Meanwhile, back at the hovel in the shaded wood, I'm getting a little restless.

I'm hungry, I need a drink, I want Alt-*Dwelobnik* in my hands. Or failing that, to know when Your Man is coming back. My story is far from told, I haven't got to Paedogate *or* my Canadian Sojourn yet. But it feels like I've been typing for years. So it'd be lovely to have an idea of when Your Man will make his return. A giant hourglass by which to gauge the time, perhaps. A sundial. A *moon* dial, maybe, since I've yet to see the sun here.

Then the hovel door blows open.

'I'm back, babes,' Your Man says. He tosses me an apple. It's not an ideal form of sustenance but I'm famished so it'll do. I catch it and throw my cigarette away. Your Man also has an apple, which he studies momentarily before he drives his massive chompers into its supple flesh. The juice spurts from the fruit and onto the thorn-hairs around his clavicle and dribbles down his tank top; his cargo shorts remain stained with mustard. I recall that earlier I smelled sausages, and deduce that Your Man is partial to hot dogs.

'You are correct, babes.'

'Ah yes – you read minds.'

'Astute of you to remember.'

'Is that a dig?'

'On the contrary.'

He bites his apple, licks his lips.

'Who *are* you?' I say.

He scrunches his nose.

'That depends.'

'On what?'

'The weathers.'

'Plural?'

'Indeed.'

'Go on.'

'The weather, as in the atmospheric conditions. But also whether I'm on or off the clock.'

'I see.'

'Of course you do.' And another crunch of his nuclear-green apple. 'You're astute.'

'Thank you, sir. As are you.'

Then there's a pause in which I remember he lied to me.

He laughs.

'*I* lied?' he says.

'Precisely.'

'Impossible, babes.'

'You did! You said you'd bring cans and Alt-*Dwelobnik* once I started telling my story.'

'If you *successfully* told your story.'

I point to my stack of pages and say, 'What is that if not success, you cunt?'

'Woah. Cool the jets, babe. We're friends?' He throws the last of the apple, core and all, into his hairy mouth. Following a few chews he spits out the pips. 'But I see your point. You've worked hard, you deserve a break. So I'll get you the goods. Back in a mo.'

While he trots away from the hovel, careful to stay within view, I take my first bites of the apple. It's tasteless and watery. He moves to the cedar, which isn't exactly as I remember, and touches the bark as though it's a fried egg whose yolk he doesn't want to break. Then he rubs it with assiduity, as if removing a stain, and knocks rapidly and at length and waits for a response. None comes. He shakes his fist, he stomps on the ground. Then his vaudeville act turns. He grips the cedar with two hands and fucks his head into it. With what, I presume, is all the energy he has in him. The bark splinters and cracks, then reveals a large hollow into which Your Man plunges his thorny and long arm. I see no blood on his forehead, not a bruise or a scratch. I do spot, however, what's different with the tree. The VS etchings are all gone, as though they had never been there. 'Who versus whom?' I want to ask. But I don't.

Your Man rummages for an age.

When he finishes, his hand emerges with a book whose back cover is missing. Ripped off, I assume, by the worst of all reprobates: those who defile literature. But it's the book that I'm after so I feel myself swoon and I wish I had a parasol and a cordial, a bonnet and a fan. All to better play my role as the overwhelmed Victorian diva. What's more, Your Man's show isn't over. He reaches again into the cavern and retrieves, with his other hand, two stubby cans.

But not cans of beer.

Or vodka sodas.

Or gin and tonics.

No.

They're …

Gosh.

Really?

'*Beans*?' I say, as Your Man canters back to the hovel.

He says nothing, just closes the door and slams the cans on my desk. He holds the book behind his back. Meanwhile, I study the cans whose aluminium casing confirms what I thought.

'Camland's finest unbranded beans,' I read. 'Marinated and pickled— Pickled? Who the hell *pickles* beans?'

In any case, this particular distributor of unbranded beans have been pickling their beans since 1979.

'You lied to me,' I say, not looking at my friend.

'I didn't, babes. Open them up.'

My hands are sticky with apple. There are no napkins in this catacomb. But because I'm still hungry, I reach for the beans. The can is lighter than I expected. I give it a rattle and hear liquid.

'That's right, babe.'

He leans close to my face, his tongue practically in my ear. Then he whispers:

'Open the beans.'

So I do.

And inside is a liquid the colour of apricots. Rimmed with a soft foam, it reflects my shocked though beautifully chiselled face.

'Drink the beans, babe.'

So I do.

And lo, it's a lager!

Or an amber ale or a pilsner!

In any case, it's *booze* and I've never been more grateful.

Then Your Man slaps the book on our rickety table and he cracks his own can and takes a deep slug.

And I see, to my delight, that the book's as I suspected.

Dwelobnik, Issue 11: 'Camland and its Discontents, Or, The Narrative That Never Ends'.

But as before in the Ussher Library, so now in the hovel: I don't want to open the journal lest it destroy this beautiful moment. I'm sipping on a beer from a can of unbranded beans, kicking it with a friend, by the fire, in a rocking chair. Who *wouldn't* want to retain the serenity of such a moment?

'Very few people, babes. But you must,' Your Man says.

And he's right.

So I flip the page.

And there it is.

Obviously, I'm ecstatic, for I was right all along. The issue does exist. But I'm also apprehensive on seeing the full list of contributors. I'm not surprised, for example, to learn that Maebh and Simone had a part to play in everything. But if that really was the case, why did Maebh and I fall out after Paedogate? And who the hell is the Pale Fella? As for the others, they're easier to countenance. There are those I once knew, those I barely met, those I've just met, or those from the dossier whose names I first saw in Gourd City. As I suspected, everyone's in on it. But J.H. McDonagh? Should it be, after so many years, that this is the manner in which I first encounter his work?

Where's Maebh Kealy when I need her for a debrief and a beer?

I reach for my can and discover the bastard's empty.

'You'll get more later, babe. In the meantime, remember why you're here: to tell your story. It's the only way you can leave. Once you do, you'll be back in the Ussher Library with Alt-*Dwelobnik* in your hands and on your way to Kenneth Connolly's death chamber of an office. And just think: how exquisite it will be to shove the journal in his face and see the dawning on his brow. You'll only impress him, however, if you can elucidate how Camland and three-dimensional narrative intersect. Not to mention how they relate to your doctoral thesis more generally. Do you think you can do that?'

'Of course.'

'But will you? You've said already that the three-dimensional narrative will determine the future of literary criticism. But have you elaborated? No. Thankfully I'm here to keep you on track. So state clearly and aloud for me what the three-dimensional narrative is.'

He prances to his rocker and takes a seat and rubs my knee. I'm not sure where all these horse metaphors are coming from, though it's probably because Your Man has the ass – and the face – of a thoroughbred stallion.

'Thank you, babe. But your theory.'

The fire crackles, the rockers groan. I stretch and flip the shoebox lid. I pinch another smoke. Light it, sip it good. I flick away my ash as though turning off the telly. Then I say:

'The three-dimensional narrative is a mercurial beast through whom—'

Your Man slaps me. Not to hurt but to daze.

'No time for floridity, my dear. Let me help you out.' He finishes the last of his can and chucks it in the fire and shoves it around with the incandescent poker. 'The three-dimensional narrative is a fundamentally sound theory, but the problem is that *you* alone could never bring it about. How could you? You're neither a novelist nor a computer programmer. But let's backtrack. What is it? An idea that in the future there will be a novel that never ends. A novel with infinite outcomes. And why is this interesting?' He stops stoking the fire and gives his nipples a quick scratch. 'Because a novel with infinite outcomes means a corpus with infinite arguments: it means an academic who's never stuck for a thesis or a job again. That's the idea, in short. And how did you form it?'

'Through graphs.'

'Correct! You drew your first graph on a stray page from Scanlon's dossier. An x and a y-axis. And under the x-axis you wrote TIME, and along the y-axis you wrote ACTION. Then you doodled. You drew a waveform. You smiled, for you saw in this waveform the shape of a story, for character is action, and it was good. But there was more. You drew a diagonal slash intersecting with your two axes, a z-axis, and alongside it you wrote OTHERS, by which you meant *other lives*, even though you were unsure what exactly this meant. Did it mean: lives that the heroine could have lived out but didn't? Or: lives that the heroine lived out in parallel universes? Or: something else, something in between, something wildly different? You never knew.'

'I still don't.'

'See! That's precisely the kind of ownership we're looking for, babes. Clarity, honesty, vulnerability, progression.'

'We?'

'You'll meet my colleagues soon. They're a hoot. For now, let's plough ahead. Because we're getting there. A slice of cheese?'

He pushes a cheeseboard towards me. I never knew it was there. But I'm glad. Understandably, I go for the brie.

'As you should,' Your Man says. 'But the z-axis. You were so close. You were right of the y-axis when you said that it operated according to morality. That positive values were good actions and negative values were evil and the further the heroine strayed from $y = 0$, the more moral or immoral her actions became.'

He takes a bite of blue cheese and spits chunks of mould while he talks.

'But the z-axis is trickier. It does indeed concern parallel lives, but not as one might expect. You, for instance, never exist on any other z-value but zero. In real life. But if this variable changed, you would become a different person in a completely different story: a Desmond, a Dorian, a Deirdre, a Dara, a Duncan, a Dooley, a Deanna and so on. With different surnames too. The value system is straightforward: negative values move into the worlds of male counterparts, while positive values move into the worlds of female counterparts. The further you get away from $z = 0$, the crazier the alternate worlds become. Thus a three-dimensional waveform, so goes your theory, results in a story that never ends. A story with infinite beginnings, middles, ends.'

'But I *know* all this. These are direct copies of my notes.'

'And yet! You can't do as I'm doing and summarise it quickly, so shut the fuck up or I'll ram my fingers up your nose.'

I feel myself flush. My gaze falls to my hands, where I see I'm holding a thin triangle of camembert. I don't remember finishing my brie, but I raise the camembert to my lips and I nibble. Your Man admires his mould-morsel, nods, then eats it.

'My spiel is all part of the procedure, babe. If I don't comply, we won't get out of here any sooner. So on that note – a question. Where the fuck are we?'

I look around the hovel. The cheese is so good I'm smiling more than I'd care to.

'In a hovel.'

'But where?'

'I can't say.'

'Of course you can't. Because you've found yourself in a unique part of the world. A place whose z-value is Not a Number.'

He taps the contents page of Alt-*Dwelobnik* and circles the final four pieces, three of whose z-values, I see, are NaN.

'What does that mean?' he says. 'Hard to explain. Unnecessary, even. So I won't. But I will say that while you are indeed in a place whose z-value is Not a Number, you also remain very much at large in the Ussher Library, where your z-value is zero and always will be. Alt-*Dwelobnik* on the other hand – that lovely specimen before you – gives the entire *range* of z-values. In so doing, it proves your theory. Just look at those contents, behold the star of the show. It's you! You're the main attraction, babes. Don't believe me? Read on. Step Two of Illumination? Address gaps in the narrative. The best part! Because you no longer have to type! You just read and log your thoughts. Then we'll revise the facts of the present day and get you back to where you belong. To the Ussher Library, to Kenneth Connolly's office. And all will be super, doll. You'll have Alt-*Dwelobnik* on your person, you'll be laughing, illuminated, free.'

This isn't what I was expecting.

Me?

The centre of Alt-*Dwelobnik*?

I was insouciant earlier, but now I feel anxiety creep back into my system. This complicates how I feel about Your Man overall. I'd love another drink, or failing that a joint, but the cheese and the fags will do for the minute. I have emptied by now a good third of the shoebox.

'No need to worry, babes. It's a spectacular achievement. You know most of the contributors, most of them know you. They all nail your voice, your biography, your tics, interests, bugbears. Then there are your parallels – the positive and negative integers – not to mention the three NaNs, which being the future have been expurgated.'

The future?

I turn over the journal, to its missing back cover, and I see the jagged margins of thirty or so torn pages.

'Most likely the Pale Fella who's responsible for that one. What a guy! But you'll live out these pages on your own time anyway. All that matters now is Step Two.'

He jerks a thumb behind his ginger bowl cut, to the sign that says, 'THREE STEPS TOWARDS ILLUMINATION'.

'A lot has happened between Paedogate and today; more than five years have elapsed. But we've taken the pressure off you. There's no writing this time. Just reading. So go slow. If you need us, we're here. Well not me. I need a nap. But the Pale Fella will be here soon. He's gas craic. And he'll have cans.'

I look down at Alt-*Dwelobnik* and I register, with forbearance, that it remains as inspiring as it was in the Ussher Library. Only where before it inspired mirth, now it freely spawns dread. Its attendant chords are no longer the major chords of choirboys but pipe-organ minors and unresolved diminished sevenths.

'It won't be the easiest read,' Your Man says. 'But it's the only way.'

And with that he rises and saunters to the door. He swings his arms gustily, and resembles a man masturbating two pensises that trail him, like little ghosts, from behind. Once outside, he climbs a white spruce that hitherto wasn't there. On its bark is etched: VS VS VS. Somehow, in a twisted position, he is comfortable among the needles. And with the door wide open, the elements again come blowing in. Then Your Man shouts:

'Make as much noise as you wish, babe! I'm the heaviest of sleepers. The Pale Fella will be with you shortly to attend to your needs. Meanwhile, recall who you really were and tell the truth for once. Address gaps in narrative.'

Then he's silent.

So I open up Alt-*Dwelobnik* and skip 'A Brief History of Camland' and I scan the first page of 'Paedogate'.

And it's unnerving, to say the least, for it picks up exactly where I stopped typing – the night I finished reading the dossier in Tiny Palace – and continues as I would have done had Your Man not returned to the hovel. The voice is mine, clear as the Angelus, the retrospective narration's the same. But how true is it that Maebh Kealy wrote this piece? Or that each 'contributor' wrote their own?

I don't know. But I need to. Because the general vibe of the forest has switched all of a sudden from Rick Astley's crooning to Bach's Toccata in D Minor.

So I do what I do best and I hole up behind words. Even though I know exactly where the story's going.

Even though I don't want it to *go* where it's going.

And to mollify my rising disquiet I pinch another piece of brie.

Paedogate

Ever the punctilious and courteous man, I returned the dossier to Scanlon the day after I read it.

But I almost didn't.

Return it, that is.

I debated heavily with myself, that morning in bed.

It was just gone 6 a.m. when I crawled under my dank sheets; I could tell by the muffled bells of St Patrick's Cathedral. When my head hit the pillow and its dried earwax and drool and many speckles of dandruff, I knew I'd never get to sleep.

So I courted sleep vainly by laying perfectly still and picturing myself on a hot day, kayaking down a river as trout swam and hemlocks swayed – my usual trick for falling asleep – but even that didn't work. I was uncomfortable, and knew why, and it had nothing to do with Camland. The real problem was that I was incapable of commitment, that I chased the rush of new things until the new was barely old and I skedaddled onto the next, until I swapped a mascu-femininity for a Camland, a Camland for a three-dimensional narrative. And even in the moment, as I failed to fall asleep, I saw for the first time who I was and would always be: someone who rotated his pastures monthly: a perpetual believer in greener grass.

But the three-dimensional narrative, I told myself, was different. Unlike Camland, it was my idea. And it was good. Theoretically, at least.

Then the bells struck 8 or 9 and Maebh got up for work. Through closed eyelids I could see light dance about the room; I liked the cast-iron glow it lit for my eyes alone. I grunted hello to Maebh, stuck out an open palm. I got what I was looking for. Two ultra-fast claps, our secret handshake of sorts. I giggled. Our handshake amused me more than it should have. Then Maebh threw a sock at me and it landed on my cheek. I couldn't tell whose it was but it was most likely mine. It was old.

'Aphrodisiacs are half price today,' she said. 'Want me to get you some?'

I snorted. Maebh worked as a store assistant at a health shop whose vitamins were sold at unhealthy prices. She was always producing good-natured dad jokes like these.

I pushed the sock off my face and opened my eyes.

'No thanks. I'll stick to beetroot smoothies.'

'Eugh.'

She shivered.

'Well you know what they say. A beetroot a day keeps ... the bukkake in play.'

'Oh my sweet fuck, Darren. Go back to bed. Forget I ever spoke, you sick fuck.'

My giggling resumed.

'Love you, sunshine,' I said.

She dug her heels into her shoes, no doubt disgruntling the Turkish barbers downstairs.

'Love you too, you orgiastic madman.'

Around noon I got out of bed and made a smoothie with Maebh's blender. Only I skipped on the beets and opted instead for banana and chia seeds and grated carrot. Maebh thought I was crazy for adding carrot to a smoothie. But try it and you'll agree that it does wonders for the skin.

While the blender screamed, I decided to locate Scanlon immediately after breakfast. Office hours be damned.

In the meantime I made a mushroom and cheese omelette and prepared what I would say to Scanlon when I saw him.

'I'm sorry, Cian,' I said aloud. 'I really can't commit to your project at the minute.'

The eggs plopped into the side bowl. I whisked them with a fork and added my signature seasoning: salt, pepper, mustard powder, cumin, tarragon, nutmeg.

'I can't healthily divide my working hours,' I continued, 'between the three-dimensional narrative, assignments, part-time bar work *and* the dissemination of information concerning an alternate Ireland, you know?'

I put my pan on low heat, tossed in a knob of butter. I swirled the gilded cholesterol juice around the entire pan. It spiralled like a coin in those old McDonald's charity bins. When it turned the colour of turmeric, I switched off the heat and set the pan aside. Then I chopped my mushrooms and my cheddar and I halved five cherry tomatoes. I chiffonaded a sprig of parsley. I folded in my eggs and the remaining ingredients as they were due.

'So I made a difficult choice, Cian. I cut out Camland, by far the weakest link.'

I ate the omelette at the kitchenette table. The dossier hadn't budged so I used a scrap of paper as a coaster. My smoothie soon made an iridescent ring stain on it.

Given the lack of sleep I'd had, I was surprised I was so content.

And I haven't eaten a more delectable omelette since.

Scanlon was delighted when I showed up at his office. So much so he pulled a box of mini-muffins from the detritus of his desk and cracked it open in my honour. He was dubious, however, about my withdrawal from Camland.

'Och, I can tell you're still interested, Darren? No need to be lying to me?'

I couldn't respond. My mouth was full of muffin and I didn't want to spray his pile of uncorrected essays with chunks of refined sugar.

'So I'll tell you what we'll do,' he said. 'You hold onto that wee dossier there and if anything tickles your fancy, you just come running on back to your Uncle Scanny and I'll set you straight.'

Uncle Scanny?

What incestuous link was he trying to establish?

Thank god for the muffin in my mouth. Otherwise, our conversation might have taken a different turn.

'Now,' he said, slapping both knees simultaneously. 'Surely there's some wee things from the folder that need ironing out?'

There were.

I swallowed the last of my mini-muffin and thought nothing more of his self-proclaimed sobriquet. I pointed to the dossier and put two questions to him.

'How many of these contributors are real and who the fuck is Harriet Farrell?'

*

Fair play to him, he told me everything I needed to know.

He hadn't written the dossier himself. It was indeed a collaborative project. He and Sophie Confey had conjured two non-identities to boost the numbers of Project Pikerowave, as he playfully pet-named the enterprise. I had already forgotten who this 'mysterious duo' were. Along with Sophie Confey. And what a Pikerowave was.

'Louise Davies and Adrian Killam are just two wee people we made up to meet our quota? Sophie is a Mathematics professor at St John's College, Cambridge? And the Pikerowave, of course, is the invention of Krickles O'Shea? Camland's entrepreneur extraordinaire? Who created an electrical appliance – part fish, part microwave – so that the resulting reheated food always tasted and smelled like freshwater pike. Ingenious, no?'

Mother of Jupity, I thought. Who *was* this man?

But it added up.

Of course Scanlon *et al.* wrote the dossier – not me, as Maebh so stonerifically suggested the night before. Of course the mysterious duo on whom I couldn't find so much as a scrap online or in the library were contrived. Of course Scanlon's project was codenamed after a ludicrous Camish businessman.

It added up.

And more to the point, if Scanlon's one-time book deal from Bloomsbury Academic was anything to go by, it added up for others too.

As for Harriet Farrell, she was another invention, though one modelled on Scanlon's niece, the forthcoming novelist Creighton Fulbright. (In the autumn of that year Fulbright would become a literary sensation on releasing the world's smallest book, *The Modern Triangle: Ending Neoliberal Mathematics*, but that's a story for another day.) Harriet Farrell was Fulbright's Camish counterpart. A cipher, Scanlon said, into whom he was going to pour the 'soul of every man and woman in Camland'. He insisted that the resultant book-length biography would ensure him a teaching position at an Oxbridge college, which was all he ever wanted in life. And though his flash-essay from the dossier didn't convince me his project was worthy of such esteem – I recall its colourless content now and I cringe – I wished him luck, for we both had the same goal: academic acclaim through a single groundbreaking tome.

As I got up, he offered me a last mini-muffin and a final interpretation of Camland.

It was, he said, a modern-day saturnalia, a show in which Irish denizens donned costumes and became better people. It was a play or an act whose foundation was self-growth. I feigned understanding, as if in some quiet epiphany, but internally I didn't buy it. Its infrastructure was too obscure for self-growth. If anything, it was self-obfuscation that Camland encapsulated.

We shook hands – his was floppy and put me in mind of wilting celery and dildos – and I left. When I came out of Rhetoric House the sun was behind the building. I stood in the shade. Magpies hopped across the GAA pitch like the jumping ball that follows words on a karaoke machine. I swung a left for the campus gates and looked at the trees, whose branches were bare but wouldn't be for much longer. On the way to Tiny Palace I concluded that Camland was a conundrum for which I couldn't readily provide answers. I expected that it offered a means by which to pierce through the multiverse, on account of the scientific titbits in the dossier, but the specifics of these means I couldn't pin down. Nor did I particularly care to. But like my newfound narrative theory, there was a quality in Camland that I was loath to dismiss as explicable under our current systems of knowledge. To truly understand it, I needed a philosophical system that no one had articulated before.

And because I was no theoretical physicist, it was time to put Camland aside.

But I was also no computer programmer. So who was I fooling?

I put my keys in the door and figurative wool in my ears.

Maebh told me she didn't want to drink that night.

*

A month of to-ing and fro-ing ensued, with no real end product. I drew graphs. Learned to code. I read a couple of Balzacs – if there was a series that came close to being endless it was *The Human Comedy* – and I tried to transpose my reading onto my theory. I shoehorned. I bluffed. I told myself I was doing fine. To unwind, I smoked cigarettes and made jalapeño margaritas. Maebh and I went to nightclubs where we slut-dropped and shifted randomers. I scissor-kicked the air. One time I knocked a guy's pint from his hand. I told him he deserved it.

'Who the fuck drinks pints in a club?' I said.

Work was uneventful. I served regulars and students alike with a blend of enthusiasm and disdain.

College was as expected. I didn't see Scanlon for several weeks. Instead I went for walks and I admired the budding leaves.

I bided my time, in other words, for the launch of *Dwelobnik*'s inaugural issue.

In late April I hopped on the 115, Bus Éireann's awful service from Mullingar to Dublin, with pit-stops along the way in Kinnegad and Maynooth.

I dropped my Leap Card on the scanner and the driver smiled like he loved me. Then I went upstairs and spent the better part of the journey staring out the north-facing window at the thrum of Maynooth's streets, the motorway birches, the shocking field of rapeseed before Liffey Valley Shopping Centre, and so on until the city, where it was just graffiti and train stations and tired businesses along the quays.

Maebh wasn't with me because she had a date with some bozo who wore plaid trousers and a clip-on nose ring. But I didn't mind.

I crossed the Ha'penny and avoided eye contact with the homeless person at the apex of the bridge. I pushed my way through a throng of Spaniards. I sidestepped Trócaire and Amnesty workers.

Soon I was at my location.

Hodges Figgis on Dawson Street.

Inside the bookshop I got loaded on bad but free wine and I looked around and totted up those I knew and might approach. There weren't many. The only one was Scanlon, who was standing between two tall women who made him look like a table-lamp. I went over because I knew none of Ireland's literati. Scanlon made eye contact, tilted his head, then one of the women introduced herself, even though she didn't need to. Her ember-red hair twirled down to her shoulders. A gap separated her front teeth. She carried herself with an air that wasn't to be fucked with. She was far too beautiful for Scanlon; there wasn't a chance the two were an item. And shaking her firm hand, I learned what I already suspected.

She was Sophie Confey, professor of Mathematics at Cambridge.

We talked a little of *Dwelobnik*, with no mention of Camland. Not at first anyway. She asked how I knew Olivia. I didn't. She thought as much, because Olivia was right beside me, on the other side of Scanlon.

Olivia O'Shaughnessy and I also shook hands before she left for the podium. When she did, Scanlon glared at me like an imp, like Martin Short's Clifford, whom I hadn't recalled since the previous November. They were both very strange men, from what I knew. And they come to me, these men, without effort on my part. They find me. They hound me.

And invariably I look away.

At the podium, Olivia tapped her microphone. The murmurs quickly died. She introduced her magazine, told some polite jokes. Under a cylinder of hard light, her features were in sharp relief. Her blonde ponytail looked like it had been scraped back with a wire brush, and her eyes were pale and green, the colour of unripe barley.

After that my mind went elsewhere. To that bog it always disembarks at after six too many drinks. A warped shitshow of a place in which at the time all is lucid and vibrant and impressing, but later is pure squalor. And yet, despite the murkiness of that night, I know everything really happened.

All of which is to say I had another three wines and went to Neary's with the others.

There, Sophie spoke a bit about Camland and was all ears for my narrative theory. She and Scanlon were just pals. 'Partners-in-crime on the old Cam-wagon!' she said. She had more gossip to divulge about the subject once she knew that *I* knew vaguely of it.

I told her of my inability to move forward with my theory. But between my umpteenth drink and a closing shot of Jemmie, we decided how I would break through my impasse.

I would combine the two, Camland and the three-dimensional narrative, since it was from the continuum of Camland (as Sophie observed) that the germ for my narrative theory emerged.

And I know – I was only away from Camland for a month and already someone had convinced me to dash back into the labyrinth.

'But before you merge them,' Sophie said, 'you'd do well to write a short piece that captures *your* sense of the Camish spirit. Otherwise your theory will always elude you. Don't believe me? Just look at these shoes.'

I looked down and saw a killer pair of green wedges. And that her toenails were painted pink.

'These are the shoes of a woman who never lies.'

I wasn't convinced. But ever one for greener grass, for jumping back and forth, I agreed to try her idea out.

'I'll help you, of course. That goes without saying,' she said. 'Meantime, get yourself home, silly.'

We said goodbye, exchanged emails, numbers, kisses. I stumbled and swayed to the Ha'penny Bridge, where I waited on the bus and spotted the 115 Guy. Even today, as I stack these pages in the hovel, I always see him around town. The first time I saw him he was also at the Ha'penny bus stop, wearing a black leather jacket, holding a Blu-ray of Fellini's *La Strada*, listening to a portable CD player via clip-on earphones. He *still* listens to CDs, even though it's 2019. I've never spoken to him. But I hope that one day I will.

On the night of *Dwelobnik*'s launch, meanwhile, more than one of us waited for the 115. We stood and shuffled in a quiet drizzle. I was exhausted and hopeful, but also paralytic. I knew I would need to listen to something obstreperous for the duration of my bus ride back to Maynooth. So that I wouldn't fall asleep and wake up in Mullingar. That had happened before. I didn't want it to happen again.

So I listened to Death Grips and channelled my inner MC Ride.

As things turned out, the resulting article almost got me expelled from Maynooth.

The hunt for the Camish Spirit was tough, I certainly wasn't prepared for the fracas that was to come, but Sophie told me she'd sort out the piece's publication once I finished writing it.

And she did.

Sort of.

Under her tutelage, I penned a satirical and anonymous article that I *thought* we were writing anonymously for *Dorset*, the student paper at Maynooth.

This turned out not to be the case.

But the article was called 'In Defence of Paedos'.

In it we made a case for the social benefits of paedophiles. It was partly an argument about free will and free speech, part suggestion that there are many worlds, in this life, of which we know nothing.

Few people were pleased by it, not least the university. Even the Physics and Mathematics departments, on whom I was relying for support, were unambiguous in their hatred of it. 'We do not and will never stand for a world in which paedophiles are a good thing,' they joint-tweeted, on behalf of the entire Sciences. 'This article is, and always will be, nothing but disgusting.'

This became their most re-tweeted and liked tweet.

It wasn't that the article's content was too sensitive for satire. Frankly it was beyond satire. The initial advocacy for child molestation notwithstanding, our readers didn't know where to start. If it was a joke, they said, it wasn't funny. If an opinion, it was barbaric. As for the projection of a future state in which paedophiles and children didn't exist, it was ridiculous. More than one perspicacious commentator noted that, in spite of its fictive quality, its formal essence was less similar to the lampoons of Jonathan Swift than to the criticism of Jean Baudrillard.

And yet, it sparked a national debate, becoming one of the few undergraduate publications in the history of the state to receive attention from national broadcasters and news firms alike. In addition to the average person on the street.

I thought at the time it was the best thing I had written. Now, in the hovel, I'm not so sure. But I still remember it by heart.

It goes a little something like this.

In Defence of Paedos

Were it not for paedophiles, society would be an overwhelmingly grim place.

Suicides would surge, murders quadruple. A sickening torpor would mortally infect culture. For the first time in history, happiness would be impossible to realise for everyone on earth.

Thankfully, this dystopia belongs yet to the future, since paedophiles remain with us. They are the rain we detest but that nourishes our crops; without them we would grow hungry. They are the jogs we go on despite our hatred of exercise; without them we would become fat. They are the personification of cod liver oil, spinach in human form, seasoning for decaying veal. To neglect them is to dissolve the glue that binds our society together.

Yet picture another future, in which the veneration of paedophiles becomes a discipline in its own right.

That's correct. Paedo Studies.

Which, after Business, will become the most popular Arts choice for Camish students whose lives lack direction. And who knows – they may become paedophiles themselves one day. Time will tell.

More certain in this future is that each human will go their entire lives with two beliefs in their hearts: that the sexual defilement of minors is not only right but good, and that the only thing more virtuous than a regular paedophile is, obviously, a cannibalistic paedophile, a breed whose type has been increasingly hard to come by.

I detect fervent cries coming from detractors already. Were I a father, they say, I would never pen such chaff. I wouldn't dare joke about a topic so sensitive and disgusting. Were I inauspicious enough to fall victim to paedophilia, were my own child snatched away, raped, murdered, eaten, I would be irrevocably heartbroken. So much so that the sight of the above words would throw me into a state so murderous that I would strangle the author were he to come within my grasp.

And these are all valid complaints.

Admittedly, I am not a father. To the agonies and ecstasies of childrearing I am oblivious. About the catastrophe of losing a child I know nothing. But I am not, as some members of the mob put it, a greater waste of breath than paedophiles themselves.

For I have a point.

If, for example, one removes children from society, one also removes the paedo. Each depends on the other.

Remove the paedo from society and little will happen. Remove the paedo *and* the child and the result will be a peculiar development in humankind, as mothers give birth not to baby girls and boys but to grown men and women. (See the work of Blue Turnip for a more detailed account of how this evolutionary change will take place.)

And because children will no longer exist, paedos will not either. Their extinction will soon follow.

But please, denizens of Camland, do what's right.

Think of the children.

In other words?

Preserve the paedo.

The article was never published anonymously in *Dorset*. It was published on my Twitter – long-since deleted – and thereafter collected by various Irish media outlets.

The furore grew, the hate spumed. Death threats poured in. Malware crept into my inbox. My lecturers refused to grade my papers, the Turkish barbers refused to cut my hair. Sophie Confey kept schtum. I emailed and I rang and I got nothing in response. Likewise for Cian Scanlon. I went to his office for support – someone threw a 99 at me on the walk over and missed – but he wasn't there. Even my family got hassle. One night a Converse shoebox appeared on their doorstep. Inside was an old baby doll across whose forehead my name was written in red ink, while through the doll's chest was a twelve-inch butcher knife.

Clearing my name was exhausting. Especially when I didn't know where I had gone wrong. I had posted the article in tweets, but I made sure to link the *Dorset* version at the beginning; Sophie emailed it to me as soon as it went live. But I got a 404 error once I went back and tried to prove that the university paper had ever published it.

Then there was the meeting with Maynooth's Board of Directors, to whom I defended my case. They had been in touch with Cian Scanlon and he had denied ever meeting me. Likewise for Sophie Confey, who hadn't been to Ireland, they said, in more than seven years, let alone last month for the *Dwelobnik* launch.

They also told me, however, that if I issued a public apology I could sit my summer exams and progress, as expected, to my final year of undergrad.

So I did.

But at Tiny Palace I fumed.

'Who's *actually* in the wrong, Maebh? Tell me. Honestly. Who?'

I was now on my fifth can of Guinness. Maebh was on Rooibos tea. She didn't answer.

'The academy! Scanlon, Simone, Sophie, Olivia. Not to mention every prick involved in Project Pikerowave. They're all laughing at me, in a pub, heating up leftovers in their giant Pikerowaves, cackling over their fish-flavoured spuds.'

'I think you *really* need a break from this Camland thing, sunshine.'

I rattled my can. It was empty.

'And maybe the booze too,' she said.

I wasn't listening. I was thinking. My logic was working overtime.

'And why?' I said. 'Because I'm *easy*. An easy target, an easy tactic. Because it's ultimately *their* game. Which is why they can abscond when I need them most. Because it's they who decide the rules.'

Then Maebh got all sentimental and started crying and called me names. She wondered when I got like this. She said I wasn't the same.

'You're telling me, Kealy. No one here is the same. Because each of you fuckers are denying your actual role. The gourds, the dossier, the emails – every one of you is fucking lying.'

I was filled with such frustration that I wanted to burn my hands, but because self-harm was never my game I directed my energies elsewhere. I grabbed the dossier and a lighter and a last can for the road. Then I left our flat and walked up Carton Avenue, a pathway lined with sycamores that leads straight to Carton House, and alongside which are rows of ditches and cubby-routes to pebbledash houses.

It was late evening by now, few were out, dusk was coming. I dipped into the ditch and tried to start a fire. But the ground was too damp so I clambered back to the avenue, where I sat on a bench and opened the dossier. I held a page from a corner and let it dangle down. Then I burned it. And another. Until the whole fucking thing was gone. Indeed, the dossier burned little but me during the few months I had spent with it. It was time for revenge. I made sure, however, to be civil. I swept the ash into the grass. I waved at late-night dog-walkers and vagrants and passersby. I gave them a smile they'd never forget.

Then I went back to Tiny Palace, where Maebh, ever the drama queen, was packing a bag and saying she didn't want to see me until I was better, whatever that meant.

After Paedogate, even Maebh hated me.

For the remainder of May she lived with the same plaid-wearing softboi whose name, I think, was Felix. So I had Tiny Palace to myself for a short while. I was knackered, I needed a cleanse, so I severed my ties with everyone. I focused on my second-year exams. I prepared essays on *Tristram Shandy* and *Northanger Abbey* and made many mushroom and cheese omelettes.

Then in June I moved home, where my parents were deeply ashamed about the whole Paedogate fiasco, and half the village too. Another rogue member of society threw a 99 at me. But unlike the Maynooth assailant, he succeeded in hitting his target. He took the flake for himself, however, which baffled me.

What else happened during the summer of 2014?

I learned to drive.

That was it.

When my exam results came in, I shoved the paper in my parents' faces. I got straight 1:1s. They didn't care.

'Didn't we expect as much?' my dad said.

After that I gave up. Only Nicholas and our dusky puckabouts were a comfort to me that summer.

I was done.

If my family didn't love me, if I had no friends in Ireland, I'd hunker down and finish my degree and emigrate on graduating.

In Maynooth that September I returned to Aoibheann Fagan, Digslord Extraordinaire. She still lived in Park Lane.

The green was a mess again.

But this time I didn't cut it.

I withdrew, I fled inward, and for a while that was enough. But soon I needed out. To escape my Camish ghosts and theoretical obsessions.

So I planned, I considered. America, Canada, Australia. Somewhere thousands of kilometres away whose official language was English. I deliberated. I decided. I worked, saved, applied.

I went through my final year as silently as I could.

Then on sitting my last exam, in May 2015, I moved to Halifax, Nova Scotia, without intending to come back for an entire twelve months. Not even for graduation that September. I went to Halifax because nobody Irish, I knew, would ever think to go there. Why would they? It was one of the few cities not advertised by MoveToCanada. com. And for that reason, I believed, I'd find no familiar faces among the province's million people.

Into my bags I packed books, clothes, hang-ups, inhibitions.

It was a time in which I thought the fulfilment of my goals was still possible.

Z = NaN

So it's true: I really am the star of the show. But I flip back to the piece's opening page, to confirm that my name isn't under the title. And it's not. It's Maebh's.

'Paedogate – Maebh Kealy', I read.

Needless to say, I have many questions.

Why would Maebh write this? *How* could she write it? Does she have access to my innermost thoughts? Why, in the piece, am I *still* typing pages in this hovel, as per Step One of Illumination? As for the remaining pieces, are they all written from this perspective? If so, what the fuck are its implications? What's the Overarching Meaning of the issue in my hands?

I have no idea. But I'm not convinced that Maebh wrote the piece. And *I* didn't write it. Or if I did, I have no memory of it. Which is worrying. And unhelpful.

I thumb, therefore, to the contributor pages for clues. Weirdly, they're at the beginning of the journal rather than at the end. This suits, because the final thirty pages have been expurgated anyway. But what I find there doesn't help. Like many from emerging writers today, Maebh's biographical note is kooky and annoying:

> Maebh Kealy is from County Sleeman. Her aphorisms have appeared on some of the finest soft drinks in the Greater Darglar Area. She is currently on trial for canslaughter, and if convicted will face the death penalty. 'Paedogate' is nevertheless her first fictional publication.

Canslaughter? What could *that* be?

Whatever the crime, I'm thinking of cans once again – and whether the Pale Fella will arrive soon – when suddenly I hear music come from outside the hovel. I know I shouldn't procrastinate, know I should keep reading and address gaps in the narrative. But the music doesn't stop, my curiosity doesn't diminish.

So I put down the journal and I scurry to the window.

To my surprise I see that, outside, the wind rustles more than bare trees; it pushes down the path large hefty pumpkins, one after the other, which skid past the hovel like tumbleweeds or plastic bags.

Gosh.

Musical gourds.

Their noise is rhythmic and melodic, the beat dotted and galloping. It comes from the smacks of the gourd-flesh on gravel. But on account of uniform gusts this rhythm is constant. And while the jumping pumpkins play what I think is a D – they sound exactly like the opening two notes of 'Sweet Home Alabama' – soon the bassline ascends, chromatically, and doesn't stop. Then more pumpkins roll in and they start over from D. The process repeats. The soundscape becomes complex. Overtones soon sound. I see a deluge of pumpkins, a motorway of gourds. I hear hundreds of notes. The ground shakes a little. I nod and smile because I'm hooked on the beat. To be sure, if art be cheese, these musical gourds are a whole wheel of Manchego, while Maebh's questionable journalism is at best a Cheestring.

Then the wind abates and so do the pumpkins.

I snap out of my reverie and recall why I'm here: to address gaps in the narrative. I understand I am no closer to fulfilling this goal than I was prior to my excessive gourd-jam, which is to say when I read 'Paedogate'.

To rectify this, I move to the table for Alt-*Dwelobnik*'s next piece.

But the procrastination continues.

For when I sit back in my rocker and prepare to read on, I notice that the fire, unfortunately, has died. There's no peat in the bucket, no kindling nor coal. Momentarily I imagine freezing to death. Then my frantic mind returns to the crime of canslaughter. Does it have anything to do with the bean-can of beer?

I can't say.

I have no idea what the felony is.

But I'd sure love another beverage.

Then the door blows open and I see fog. That's new. But I also see a flaxen and gaunt type who's sporting a long cowl. His face is neither so bland as to be unnoticeable, nor so distinct as to be wholly memorable. I regret to see he's another man. On his triangular face are rose-gold glasses and the repellent blemishes of someone old enough to know better, like how to take care of his skin, while his sable cowl is less a hood than a cloak. It extends to his ankles. On his feet are battered black plimsolls, from which hairy toes protrude. Though he tries his best to scowl, he doesn't quite succeed. Above all, he is pallid.

He is an epilogue of a man.

Then he opens his right hand, in which is a tiny and mouldy pumpkin. From his body language it's clear he doesn't want to come in. That he wants me to stand up and address him.

So I do.

I point. I crouch slightly and I say:

'The Pale Fella?'

'That is me, comrade.'

'And have you cans?'

'That I do.'

'So ... may I have one?'

'You may. But first we must gather fuel.'

He gestures for me to join him outside.

So I do.

We go only thirty yards from the hovel. The Pale Fella gestures for me to keep quiet, since Your Man snoozes above us, in his spruce tree, the lazy boyo. I want to say that if he slept through the fortissimo pumpkins, he'll sleep through our conversation. But I don't. I walk and crunch snow.

I keep quiet until we reach our destination. It's a ten-foot pyramid made from a thousand tiny pumpkins. They're the same as the one in the Pale Fella's hand. Each is mouldy as hell, as if they've been sleeping with Your Man's blue cheese. I wonder if they're the same pumpkins whose enchanting music I heard earlier. But they couldn't be, for each pumpkin is at least a tenth of the size.

Their smell is foul.

'Oh my god,' I say. 'That's foul.'

'No worse than you're used to, comrade.'

I don't know what to make of this. Then he hands me a pail. Where from Jesus knows.

'Pick a gourd, any gourd.'

I comply.

'Good man. Repeat the process. Fill your pail. I'll do the same. And when we're done, what'll we have?'

'Two large buckets of pumpkins, sir.'

'No, comrade. Not quite. Two large buckets of *pumpkinettas*. They're different, see?' He puts one in my hand. 'But more than that, we'll have fuel.'

To demonstrate, he reaches into his cowl-pocket and pulls out a box of matches and lights the pumpkinetta on which he rolled into town. Though he burns himself in the process, he makes his case clear: the pumpkinetta is a Grade-A Combustible, a most efficacious fuel. Then he extinguishes the flaming gourd by driving it into the snow. With his plimsoll and hairy toes.

He offers me a smoke and, because mine are in the shoebox, I accept, ignite, inhale.

It's a Marlboro Light. But I won't hold it against him.

We smoke while we work, we fill our pails in silence.

Once back in the hovel we encounter a slight change in furniture.

Gone are the rockers. In their place are camp chairs. In the cupholders are cans down which perspiration drips. They are tins of Galahad, a blast from a messy past. Under the circular window is a cooler in which are more cans of Galahad. The Pale Fella and I load the hearth up with gourds. We start a new fire. We slide into our camp chairs. We rip into our cans of lager and toast, thankfully, to nothing.

Because the Pale Fella is silent, I don't know what to make of him. Instinctively I'm suspicious, and for this I blame his cloak, since its sable hue reminds me of my father's curly hair. Even with the door closed and the fire screaming he says nothing.

But I know this moment won't last, so I kick back for the minute and I savour my cheap lager.

*

Eventually, he speaks.

'Now Darren,' he says, lightly animated all of a sudden. I suspect he might be drunk. 'We both know why you're here. You're in a spot of bother, you need a nudge in the right direction. And that's fine. Nothing wrong with a little help now and then. In fact, we all need it. But the line of business Your Man and I are in? The company we represent? We're not in the game of ending things early. Or prematurely. Never, never, never. At least, not when we have a say in the matter.'

He hands me another can and sits down in his camp chair.

I don't recall his standing up.

He carries on.

'I'll be the first to admit, however, that Your Man is a dickhead. Manipulative, egomaniacal, dem—'

'Oi. Leave him out of this. I'm rather fond of the prickly bastard.'

'Of course you are. Because you're a terrible judge of character.'

'That's very rude of you to say, Mr Pale Fella.'

He ignores me.

'My point is that, even when he's lying, Your Man is rarely wrong. Because the company we represent are not ones to *sell* fibs, only to rectify them. Which brings us to your case.'

We take a breather to gulp booze. There are glugs and dual-tone sighs. Then the Pale Fella goes:

'So here's what we'll do. We'll have an auld sup and we'll buckle down to work. If Your Man has you bothered, just forget about him for a few hours. You're with me now. And look at me, yeah?'

He spreads his arms wide, like the Vitruvian Man's.

'I wear a cowl, for fuck's sake. I'm far cooler than any hedgehog-fucking, tanktop-wearing, tree-hopping *Mícheál*, if you haven't noticed already.'

I don't believe him.

'You don't have to, comrade. Just listen. Your lies so far have mostly been those of omission. In other words they're no biggies, they're

119

easily addressed. They're also, I know, a current cause for anxiety, which the musical gourds temporarily erased from your disposition. So let's break it down. You read the next piece in Alt-*Dwelobnik* and I'll let you in on a little secret.'

I don't like him, but I'm enticed.

'Good man,' he says. 'We're not asking for much. Ownership, vulnerability, clarity, progression. Own it so and let me hear that boyo sing.'

I had never known it was possible to exist in a world where tiny pumpkins make for great fuel, and giant pumpkins for hypnotic music; a world where self-knowledge feeds a mysterious game, where cowls and plimsolls are a sign of exquisite style. I hadn't questioned it earlier, I sunk into its seduction, but in the Pale Fella's presence I wonder for the first time whether this is, in fact, a benevolent forest I'm in.

'You'll find out very soon, comrade. And not to flog a dead horse, but what Your Man says is true. We *will* get you back to the Ussher Library, to Kenneth's office. But what we need *first* is for you to fulfil your contract. Sing for me then your true experience in Canada. Sing for me, good man that you are, your Henry Street Blues.'

From his cowl pocket he whips out a portable CD player. He has matching clip-on earphones, which he attaches to his head. The same as the 115 Guy's. He leans back, presses play, closes his eyes, smiles. His earphones leak enough sound for me to detect who's playing.

Rick Astley.

So before I start the next piece I give my rear deltoid a pat and I applaud my observational prowess from earlier.

Then I start Simone Longford's 'Henry Street Blues'.

And all the while I tell myself that everything will be fine.

Henry Street Blues

On finishing my final-year exams, in which I truly outdid myself, I relocated to Canada in the summer of 2015. My sole intention was to write and travel coast to coast in a deadbeat wagon and burn it in the woods. To start a bushfire and fly back to Dublin from Vancouver.

No, I jest.

I'd make a terrible arsonist.

I could never handle the heat rashes.

In Nova Scotia I lingered longer than I intended. I fell into a relationship almost as quick as it fizzled out. That, for the most part, took up most of my time in Halifax. And dodging phone calls from my father, guilt-bombs from my mother (bookended with obscure emojis) and the occasional passive-aggressive email from Nick, who'd just got his first laptop. Not to mention casual sex with married men. There was a lot of that in Canada.

I had a two-year visa and 200,000 words in jottings. There was no point in going home. Better to use my Canadian sojourn, I reasoned, to assemble a draft of my theory and then return to the *fáda*-land for postgraduate research in earnest. I had deferred an MPhil at Trinity just before I left. Literature of the Americas.

Meanwhile, my family texted. Insinuated. Coaxed. Or tried to, anyway, by saying they were hurt. But what did that mean?

That they wanted me to come home so they could look down on me from a distance. That's what it meant. It always had, always would.

So I stayed put in Nova Scotia.

In Halifax, however, things were no better. I grew anxious since it wasn't a place I could call home. It felt nameless and spaceless. An underscore of a city. And yet I knew what it was.

This was Mi'kma'ki, a tiny piece of Turtle Island, soil for which many were right to still mourn. On which imperialism was reproached but unconsciously celebrated by many. At plays, gatherings and ceremonies, those in charge would acknowledge that we were standing on unsurrendered Mi'kmaw territory. But in order to become a Canadian citizen, you had to swear allegiance to the British Crown. Queen Elizabeth smiled from every twenty-dollar bill. Union Jacks, as far as I could see, were common business logos around the Maritimes.

And yet, for all I recognised the legitimacy of Nova Scotian culture, I cared little for it. I was het up, rather, because I was wedged between the ass-cheeks of the past. Though I left Ireland to escape the mechanics it was run by and under, in Halifax my condition was similar. I was always one step away from enlightenment and happiness.

From thinking I knew what was wrong with me. In Ireland, I believed I needed total anonymity, while in Nova Scotia it was the province's inner being that I wanted, since everyone around me seemed happy within it.

But whenever I sought it, two main things happened.

I lapsed into stereotypes, I drank Oland's and Keith's. I said 'Keep your stick on the ice' and visited Luckett Vineyards. I stayed away from the black rocks at Peggy's Cove.

Or I saw Irish ghosts. Doppelgangers, memories, sentences, images. All manifested in unique and mysterious ways to confound me further.

Why the fuck was I really here? What the fuck was I really missing? What was I doing working in a petrol station over 4,000 kilometres from Ireland, in a place where the cost of living was significantly higher than in Maynooth?

What was I looking for?

The answer, of course, had nothing to do with the three-dimensional narrative and everything to do with my mother.

She wasn't well.

In the year prior to my departure, she had burned family albums and cried for the same albums. She had tried to steal a neighbour's car. She thrashed the house and in the resulting remorse was so overwhelmed that she slashed one of her palms while paring potatoes. She walked to Mullingar where, despite hating spirits, she downed a half-bottle of Powers; when we found her, she had an arm wrapped around the Joe Dolan statue and was singing 'I Need You' to mackintosh-clad tourists who thought she was an actor. She recorded videos on her phone in which she asked the camera why neither of her sons loved her. I never understood this one. Nicholas still lived at home, while my birthday cards always made her cry. Even if what I said was all platitude.

That was a year ago, and in Canada things were … ?

Worse, frankly. When I left she was no longer working. Ger was doing half-days to be around her more often. She would freak out otherwise. But I knew it was all an act. That she was doing it for the attention. Her every text was an attempt at manipulation, to get me back to Ireland and absolve her of her wrongs.

She wanted the same thing I had wanted when I was young and vulnerable: constant attention and praise. And now that the roles had flipped, I knew how best to strengthen our relationship. I'd treat her with neglect for the most part, but compassion every so often, and eventually when I returned we'd put a stop to our oscillations. We'd complete the game and move on.

Meanwhile, we needed a break from each other.

It was a sound idea.

Or so I thought.

'Hi Dar, was cleaning the attic today and found this cutie pie. Give us a call to know you've landed safe? Xxx'.

I arrived at Stanfield Airport three hours before this text. I knew my parents would have already checked online to see if I made it to Nova Scotia. So there was no point in replying. It was bait. Nothing else.

Attached to the text was a photo of my old teddy, a stuffed fox I called Fig Roll, who had a smile on him like a scimitar and a bib that said FOXIE.

If this was what my mother was sending on day one, I didn't want to know what it would be like later on.

I deleted the photo, which my photo gallery had cached, and left the message on read.

I took work where it came. The more menial the better. I didn't apply to bars since the hours and the drinking interfered heavily with my writing. The first job to arrive was a night shift on Quinpool Street, not far from where I lived.

Isaac Buell was no looker. He had the skin tone of a turnip. Harsh purples and phlegm yellows. The first time I saw him I thought he had been attacked. His cheeks were puffy and bleeding and he had alarmingly few teeth. I learned later that he just drank a lot. Which explained it. And how, during the interview, he told me he hadn't brushed his teeth in thirty-two years.

'Saved some two thousand dollars on toothpaste, I reckon.'

'No kidding?'

Nodding, he looked out the window and studied the forecourt with rheumy eyes. I didn't think the price was worth boasting about. But I needed the work, so I said nothing of the sort.

I do Nova Scotians a disservice by beginning with Isaac Buell, my Stage Maritimer. All the same I encountered him, he was real, these are the facts. Even if I don't know how a hick like him ended up in the city.

But as managers go he wasn't the worst.

'Hi Dar, just wondering if you're okay or need anything, loads happening here, miss you lots. I've planted butternut squash, did I tell you?? Dad's sciatica is back. Call me love you BYE xxxx'.

Then a photo of the garden and a new patch of soil in which, I presumed, butternut squash seeds were germinating.

I deleted the photo and left the message on read.

Within weeks, Isaac promoted me to evenings. 5–11 shifts. Mostly on my own. Sometimes with his son Reggie, the store's stay-at-home supervisor. This was in late June.

Reggie lived upstairs in a bachelor apartment, beside the closet where we kept the coffee cups and wooden stirrers. He had a chipped front tooth and a humble attitude. Though there were few things he wouldn't do, 7 a.m. starts was one of them. For the most part he sauntered down at noon, held the fort, went back upstairs at eight. He had a trumpet, he told me, that he never played anymore.

Shortly after I met him, he said he'd show me around. I was relatively familiar by then with the neighbourhood and the surroundings. I'd been living in Halifax for five weeks, I had walked most of the city. But I knew very few people and was more lonely than I let on. I therefore agreed to the walk.

While we strolled, Reggie held a small Tupperware container in which a slice of Black Forest ham lay on two Wonder bread chunks. Not much of a tour guide, he reeled off what he saw, his voice adenoidal and conceited. He read the signs of the shops that flanked our bored eyes. He spat through his teeth. Between lazy bites and words. Passersby looked at me as if I were responsible for him. I grimaced, mouthed apologies. Meanwhile I wondered how Reggie came to possess such a high opinion of himself. I concluded it most likely had to do with him being a white man.

'Korean BBQ,' he said. 'United Baptist Church. Greek restaurant. Bagels. Crappy Tire. Booze. Superstore. Cross here.' And a wet bite of his sandwich. 'Starbucks. And that's it, really. That's Quinpool, buddy.'

The majority of Nova Scotians I knew were not like the Buells at all.

'The least you could do is text.'

My father, ever the solicitor, always ended his texts with a period.

That was just one way how you knew he was a cunt.

I left the message on read.

I lived on Henry Street in a weather-worn duplex. The garden was a mess. There were lilacs but that was it. Otherwise it was just weeds. Ten-foot, two-foot, they were everywhere.

I didn't feel like replicating my landscaping stunt from Park Lane because I knew no one would thank me.

Kyle was the worst roommate I had, not because he always wanted to play Twister, nor because he insisted I learn the bass part for 'Sex on Fire' and join a Kings of Leon covers band. He wasn't loathsome because he clipped his toenails on the coffee table, nor because he once left a pot of Kraft Dinner by the bathtub. (With water, and what appeared to be jizz, still lingering in the tub.) He was insufferable because of his remorseless capacity to inflict tedium among those he lived with.

He worked in the Navy. 7–3 shifts each morning. When he heard movement he pounced. Were I in the kitchen to make tea he'd appear from his bedroom and seize me for conversation. Only it was less a colloquy than a barrage in which he unloaded from work and other aspects of his dreary life. His back problems. His ex, who stole his beagle three years ago. His antipathy for the city of Halifax in comparison to that bastion of civilisation, his hometown, Vancouver. He looked and acted like an ugly dog that fit and yelped in a purse. Crew cut, beady eyes. Twink-like proportions. Skin so tanned he could pass for an indigenous person, a Latin American, an Italian, an Asian man. He had ties, he told me, to all these ethnicities.

My other roommate was tolerant, if docile. We bonded primarily through our mutual disdain of Kyle.

Ben was shy. Had Kyle not been our roommate we would have had nothing to talk about. A Geography student at Dalhousie University, he worked at a company for whom he compiled sports statistics. He was short, like a penguin; his face displayed at all times a promise of happiness, as if he didn't have it then but one day he'd find it. He always ate apples.

There were few days on which we genuinely wanted to talk, and only one instance in which I made Ben laugh. I had just revealed the varying grades of stupidity of which I was capable, and which I flaunted that week running errands before work.

'So,' I said. 'I needed beans, ground beans, since I have but a French press and we don't have a grinder. I pop into The Other Bean. Before work. Hooray. Only when I go in, my glasses steam up on account of the weather. I'm awkward. I remove my glasses. But don't you know, I can't see. I shuffle to the stand where sit the beans. Lo, my sight is near blindness. The vibes are not good, the vibes are in fact bad. I suspect the barista is looking at me and, ever Canadian, wants to help. I plough ahead, keep low. I find a medium-sized bag of dark-roast whole beans. Fuck. Another scan of the stand reveals they *only* have whole beans. I look over at buddy. "Do you, good sir, have any ground beans?" "No," he says. "But I can grind anything you want. It'll only take, like, thirty seconds." Perfect. Life is good again, Ben. The balance of the universe is restored. However – and this is where everything goes to shit – buddy picks up the bag that I've placed on the counter. Then he goes, "How d'you make your coffee?" And I, being me, instinctively tell the truth: "Uh … with milk?" And he laughs. The bastard *laughs* at me. "Noooo, I meant with what *machine*?" And immediately it hits me and I apologise and say French press and he grinds my damn beans and I shake my head, afterwards, for what feels like my whole shift.'

There was a long and garbled text in which my mother said she was sad. But I knew she wasn't serious. That she was in the living room, on the recliner, watching *Casualty*, drinking tea.

Attached was a photo of me as toddler. I studied my former self. I was wearing aviator shades, a nappy, a T-shirt on which a sun smiled, and a camouflage bucket hat. In my hand was a can of Beck's.

I deleted the photo and left the message on read.

But I rang my mother and, as I suspected, she was fine.

'There's nothing wrong then?' I said.

'Well, we really miss you.'

'But nothing's *wrong*?'

'Are you not hearing what I'm saying?'

'I am. But I don't believe you.'

'We love you, petal.'

'I don't have time for this. I'm late for work.'

'Hold on. I need you to say it, lovey.'

'Say what?'

'That you heard me say we love you.'

I was silent.

'Please,' she said. 'For me?'

'I gotta bounce. Enjoy *Casualty*.'

And that was the last time I spoke to my mother on the phone.

By week six or seven, I was flooded with desire. Not to fuck but be fucked. To grip a dick in my hands and ease it up my lubed sphincter. Certainly, it had been a while. I hadn't been with a man in over a year, despite the fact that men dominated my life. I had few female contacts; my co-workers and roommates a case in point. And yet, for all I wanted a seven-inch horn in me, I craved equally to escape my male-heavy landscape.

Even now, as I stack these pages in the hovel, I see the worst in my sex, see that we're an inherently filthy specimen. And though women aren't much better, men make me want to break and eat glass until the shards pierce my organs and I bleed out for all to see. But instead I fuck and serial-date. I consult Grindr for pricks and Tinder for kicks. I seek queer oblivion as much as doomed hetero partners.

But as in Ireland, so in Canada: these romantic incursions didn't in any way last. I pandered to them periodically, as though they were seasonal, bi-yearly or annual feast days and they followed the same schedule. There was usually a week-long interlude during which my chakras aligned perfectly. Bliss preceded pain. Orgasm, breakup. And by that point I was more of a mess than I was to begin with.

I treated sex then in two ways: as a meaningless exchange of free goods or as a means to simulate intimate connections. In the latter I never had much luck or experience, but it's the only reason why I pursued Canadian partners as I did. To find someone in whose company my outlandish ideas were inconsequential.

That's how I met Hannah.

*

We matched on an app and speedily arranged a walk, in Point Pleasant Park, where there was a colonial redoubt and a view of the harbour and its varicoloured cargo containers and cranes.

In the park, Hannah said she perceived in me a dark force. Those were her exact words. I laughed, then asked her to say the words again.

'I perceive in you a dark force.'

I could see her scalp in the sunlight, her hair little more than a crew cut. She had shaved it a month ago. She wore tortoiseshell sunglasses and had eczema in her ears.

'That's a new one,' I said.

'It's not funny.'

'No?'

She shook her head.

'You hide things.'

'Like what?'

She couldn't say.

'The darkness does you no favours, Darren. It never does.'

'It saves money on sun cream. That's a favour. Look how pale I am.'

'Don't joke. What are you hiding?'

She was crazy. But she was hot and I was horny so I persisted, I played along.

'I think we need a drink if we're going to continue this conversation.'

I've never had any doubts that I'm the centre of my relationships. That I'm more important than the other. I could say my partners are to blame for my interpersonal failures. Could say I'm avoiding Hannah as a subject because I respect her as a person, because I don't have her consent to speak of her with candour. But the reality is I'm too selfish. I'm compelled to talk, rather, about the feelings she stirred in me, since they're ultimately what prompted me to up sticks to Manitoba. And later, to come *back* from Manitoba. And though I feel some compunction about my egotistical nature, it remains only slight. It's something I've grown to live with. But for entertainment's sake, for my own, for Illumination, I'll do my bit and sketch her out a little further.

Most days Hannah and I hung out in the city. She worked in Truro – Nova Scotia's largest town – at a camp whose summer schedule was so intense as to preclude the possibility of a social life until the school year started back. I don't know why I was with someone who lived an hour out of the city. For the four months we semi-dated, we considered ourselves exclusive for a whole three weeks. She had a sex friend who she said was vanilla, a guy with an attainable dick. He came around once in a while and when he did they had nothing to talk about. They watched YouTube videos of Bob Ross and *Jeopardy*. They ate peanut M&Ms and had sex so tepid that it would never get better no matter how many toys or positions were involved.

On hearing this, I knew we wouldn't work out. Peanut M&Ms were never something I could get behind.

She also told me what I didn't want to hear. That was another reason we didn't work out.

'Your theory's a mess, Wally. Can't you see that?'

She remains the only person to ever call me Wally.

This was in my bedroom, on Henry Street, where the floorboards matched the bedsheets and the fly screen was warped and cracked. It was common for us to wake up with mosquito bites. Or to the invisible, incessant pinches of my least favourite fly, the no-see-um. Like an army of tiny tanks, the no-see-ums came in hordes and resisted your every swat, and the minute they woke you your snooze was as good as over.

'The only way it'll work,' Hannah continued, 'is if first you write a novel and then re-write its every action until you have thousands or millions of novels.'

'I know.'

'And will you do that?'

'Probably not.'

I was high on an edible, sitting on a chair with wonky caster wheels, wrestling my foot into a sock. Hannah was topless, on my bed, rolling the wet plastic swivel-ball of a deodorant stick under her armpit.

'Do you have any aspiration to write a novel, even?'

'I do not.'

'Then give it up.'

So I did.

On both my sock-wrestling and the three-dimensional narrative.

It was that easy.

I forgot about my family and threw myself into sex.

For all my bisexual leanings, I wanted to make up my mind. I wanted, on the one hand, a monogamous relationship, preferably one that lasted longer than six months. How nice it might be, I thought on better days, to have some sort of amorous stability, a token by which to appease Venus or Aphrodite or whatever we call her these days. The flipside was that I wanted nothing other than to fuck my life away. To be consumed in one sexual act so potent and vile as to make me think *Never. Never again will I fuck or be fucked.* To reach that extreme point from which I might never come back.

While this kind of fantasy didn't present itself, there were several places in Halifax where I could procure sex with ease.

The first was Citadel Hill, the city's prime spot for cruising. Before long, at night, a window rolled down. The rest, following the right kind of eye contact and conversation, was straightforward and consensual. No one asked for directions. No police that I knew of charged men with soliciting.

More special, however, was Scotia Sailors, a bathhouse on Brunswick Street. There was a hot tub, naturally. But deeper into its lair were a sex swing and glory holes and darkrooms for straights, portholes for voyeurs, and normally lighted rooms in which to fuck freely without strings.

The only money I spent was on tips, towels and locker keys. And Twinkies from the vending machine. To attract younger numbers, the management offered free lockers to students. I couldn't tell if their promotion was successful. Those from my demographic tended to avoid it. Only creepy old men went to it anyway, they said.

But I thought it was lovely and beautiful and pristine. The first time I visited, seven guys grabbed my cock. Not one said a word. It was ideal. Nothing fancy. Certainly nothing financial. Just a space in which to enjoy wordless sex.

And as a physiotherapist fucked me over a leatherette massage table, I wondered whether the same system could ever work for cishets.

There was a month or so in which I never heard from my family.

I assumed they were mirroring my own strategies.

When Hannah wasn't around, which accounted for most of the time, I took long walks around Halifax to acquaint myself with the area. I left my phone and my wallet at home. I perused street signs as I went and returned slowly to my residence. I enjoyed knowing that if I wanted to, I could walk into a stranger's house. Though some Haligonians locked their doors, many didn't. What would they say if I walked into their kitchen, just to ask how they were doing? Would they strike me, call the police? Would they shepherd me to the street? I wasn't willing to find out, to let my curiosity override my more rational personality. Instead I long-wayed towards Henry Street, to our hirsute back garden, while thinking about Halifax, what it was or might be. I pinned down several shit answers for a *Jeopardy* episode that Hannah and her sex friend had yet to see.

Halifax, I thought, was a black denim jacket whose back read CARLING BEER. Halifax was 'Bohemian Rhapsody' at the Lower

Deck on a Sunday night. Halifax were these streets: Cunard, Maynard, Agricola, Robie, Charles, Windsor; foreign names whose significance I hadn't yet assimilated, whose people I served regularly on Quinpool but otherwise couldn't see. I would *never* have access to the private, unconscious culture. The slang shied from my lips, the ancestry was beyond my knowledge. The classrooms I couldn't picture. Whom did one support in hockey, and why? What were the university stereotypes and their paired hangout spots? Where could I find the cheapest pint? (It was a while before I learned it was something of a three-way tie between Split Crow, during Power Hour, Oasis and the Local.) I walked up and down the roads in the neighbourhood. Walnut, Chestnut, Larch, Jubilee, Watt. I looked up at the houses that were all made of wood – where were the bricks? – and felt nostalgic for housing estates, cul-de-sacs, boreens, ditches. Then I laughed at my foolishness, for I was now the gobshite who went abroad and was surprised that things were different. And yet, though I removed my shoes at the door and kicked them into the boot tray, I wouldn't call this place home. I wouldn't gift it that worth.

In between my walks, I was steadily working away. I had given up on the three-dimensional narrative and was thinking, again, about Camland. At the petrol station, I told Isaac and Reggie what I remembered from the dossier. They thought I was summarising a TV show. So too the bar staff at Radley's, on whom I unleashed my spiel. They were used to my ravings because I popped in for a pint and a burger most days on my break, then came back later and stayed on into the night.

Elsewhere all was flat. I saw nothing of merit in adults, children, animals. Or the natural world. Once again, Camland existed as a refuge of sorts. I lived there as much as in Canada, then as much as now. It was as if I couldn't catch up on the present. I began to doubt my life decisions. I questioned every idea I ever had. Was there *ever* something of worth in my thoughts, now or then? Something on which the death of capitalism could play out? Or the future of literature unfold?

As usual, I didn't know.

But as autumn came and went, I remembered something Hannah said during our first pint about 'my darkness'.

'You should go north,' she had said.

'Why?'

She didn't know.

'Have *you* been north?' I said

'No.'

'Seems counter-intuitive.'

'Then go south.'

I laughed.

'Go east or west, even.'

I finished my Galaxy and ordered us another round. She was a weird fish, Hannah McAllister.

But from then on I knew I'd go north sooner or later.

'Dar, do you remember this??? Playing now and missing you xxx'.

The photo was of a walnut slab onto which a circle, a triangle, a pentagon and a hexagon were drawn in permanent black marker.

Good ol' Jupity.

But their set-up was all wrong. The pawn-coins were in the wrong place.

I kept the cached photo but I left the message on read.

As always in my case, I grew sick of my surroundings and the only solution was to leave. With Hannah and me finished – another disaster into which I'm not willing to go any further – and me banned from Scotia Sailors, there was no reason to stay. For the six or nine months more I was planning to stay in Canada, I wanted an opportunity to leave behind my former self. I wanted to kill him off. I craved an inhospitable environment in which to bury the three-dimensional narrative before I flew back to Ireland.

To that end I secured a six-month teaching position in Churchill, Manitoba. I left on January 2, 2016. I started work the following week. I sent final texts to my family and said I would be offline for six months. If they needed me for emergencies, they could find me via a friend. I gave them a number but I made an effort to be untraceable. The number belonged to Reggie, whom I told I was moving to New Brunswick. And though Isaac, acting as my referee, spoke to the principal at the Earl of York, he also didn't probe enough to know where I was really off to.

No one in Nova Scotia had a clue where I was going.

Before leaving, I donated my phone and laptop to the Salvation Army. On the bus to the airport I saw two dead racoons and a flaming truck in which I imagined a family had burned slowly to death. The thought was comforting.

I welcomed the carnage, I let horror in.

I couldn't shake the sense that something horrific would soon befall me.

Z = NaN

As with 'Paedogate', so with 'Henry Street Blues'.

Why would Simone Longford have written this? *How* could she have written it?

I look to the window as though the answer were outside, where Your Man snoozes still, and I hear his sharp band-saw breaths. Though out of view, he is up there, among the needles. He hasn't budged a bit from the comfort of his spruce tree.

The Pale Fella and I go can for can, meanwhile, as he listens to Rick Astley; his cowl is effectively a bottomless pit of CDs. I set Alt-*Dwelobnik* on the table because I have a question I want answered, though it has less to do with Simone's knowledge of my Canadian

Sojourn than with the Pale Fella's secret that he promised to tell me earlier.

I have mixed feelings about him, so when I get up for another can it's as if the alcohol were a flame and the quietude were a match. But the only bangers here are gourds, those poor pumpkinettas whose flesh is chewed by many worms, and which periodically we toss onto the malodorous fire. The gourds crackle like honeycomb and jizz sparks in our general direction. I hadn't expected them to be as feisty as they are.

I poke the Pale Fella with a can and his closed eyelids unroll and his Vaseline-green eyes appear like a bowling ball from the floorboards.

'Your secret,' I say.

He pauses his CD player and unclips his earphones.

'What you say, comrade?'

'Your *secret*.'

'Ahz, yessum. My secret.'

Giggling, he stretches for the closest bucket of pumpkinettas. The rear legs of his camp chair come off the ground and wobble. He almost falls into the pail. He's hammered, I infer, though he's only had six cans. Then he corrects the chair's balance and scoops a gourd and eats it.

I hadn't known the pumpkinettas were edible, but they sound dense and most unappetising. The Pale Fella chews furiously. I'm surprised his teeth don't shatter. I slouch into my camp chair and look towards the window. Beyond it there's only darkness. I can't even see the trees. And yet the etchings come to mind. VS VS VS. Who versus whom. Beech, cedar, spruce. The Pale Fella stares me down for the duration of his chewing, his eyes googly with the booze. He does so for so long as to give me a case of the heebie jeebies.

I reach for a fag because it's been a while since I smoked. Maybe that's why I'm on edge – not because the Pale Fella munches loudly with an open mouth. The nicotine is manna to my fulsome lungs; they wheeze in thanks with each crisp inhalation. I pat the shoebox thrice, though I'm still craving a joint. Then the Pale Fella, finally, swallows his pumpkinettas and starts speaking.

'What's difference, comrade?'

'Between me and you?'

'Your Man and me.'

I think about it.

'Your clothes.'

'No no *no* no no.'

'Your hair?'

'Nopesie.'

He hiccups.

'Your career goals?'

'N— Astually, in a ways, yes. Goods for you?'

'Thank you.'

He opens his seventh can. I'll have to cut him off after this because I don't want to clean his vomit.

'I'm an agency worker?' he says.

'That better not be your secret.'

'Nopesie? But it means I care less for this job than Your Man does. Got it?'

'Understood.'

'Alls of which means that today is my last shift and you're my last client.'

I choose not to point out the lack of causality between his sentences. I don't like him. He's an idiot. I can't wait for him to fuck off and leave me alone with Alt-*Dwelobnik*.

'And I will, comrade. But my secrets is that, for your benefit, I'm gonna go a little *off script*. Off-road. Like a meat wagon in the desert.'

He raises both hands as though surfing gnarly waves.

I'm unsure what a meat wagon is, or why it might be unusual to find one in a desert, but I don't like where he's headed. For his words are delivered with the clear timbre of Dutch courage. With the portentous enunciation of someone who knows that what he's about to say is dangerous.

He clears his throat.

'I don't cares if I tell the truthums, because you deserve to know the truthums? And – whoopsie-lee! – no one can fire me if I do.'

He looks at me as if summoning what's left of his sobriety.

'The secrets is that Your Man and me? Everyone heres? We're all in your head. None of us is real.'

And though I don't believe a word he says – who could ever believe a drunkard like him? – in no way do his sentences stir up good feelings inside of me.

'You're mad,' he says. 'It's simplicious. Just look around. Musical pumpkins? Shapeshifting trees?' He belches. 'Excuse me.'

I laugh. I'm not worried. Me? I laugh again.

'But Your Man—'

'Your Man's *lying*, Darren. Just as you're lyings to yourself and avoiding Manitoba.'

I know he's talking drivel but at the mention of Manitoba I feel my stomach become a swamp in which I writhe and sink and drown. And instinctively I'm humming; a foolish, childish gesture. But momentarily it works and he's silent and I'm in control. I'm actually golden? I hum and scat and toss my cigarette on the fire. Then I light a new one and sip my beer.

'Your lifes is fucked up, comrade. Will you please admit that? Finallys?'

'I'll admit I find it rich that a dipsomaniac like yourself is casting aspersions on *my* life.'

'Ditch the lingo, Bingo!' He takes a sip from his seventh can.

140

'It won't saves you now. But what just might is if you accepts that Camland and your theory will never *ever* make sense.'

This goes against everything Your Man has said, obviously, so I gesture to Alt-*Dwelobnik*.

'Then why would other people have written this?'

'They didn't! *You* did.'

I scoff.

'When would—'

'Today, yesterday, whenever. Does it matter? No. What matters is you can't admit it. Just as you can't admits that most of the thing's *blank*.'

Then he leans over and opens Alt-*Dwelobnik* on, to be sure, a blank page. So I go back to the beginning and rifle through the whole thing. I see the title and the contents pages, the contributor notes, 'Paedogate'. I see 'Henry Street Blues' and 'Manitoba Dreaming'.

Then there are a hundred or so blank pages.

And finally 'Begad, Kinnegad!', which ends mid-sentence where the journal is ripped off.

'Where's the rest?' I say.

'It doesn't matter, comrade. It's all nonsense. Won't you finally admit that now?'

I don't know what to say or where to look.

'Look at the *journal*, buddy. Because we're going backs to Manitobas.'

My swamp of a stomach opens up again and swallows me.

'Because what's the single biggest truth you *still* can't admit, comrade?'

I want nothing more than for Your Man to escort this gentlemen off the premises. I wish I had a little countertop bell with which to wake him up.

'Hey? Stop evading. What's the biggest gap, *brother*?'

'I don't know what you're talking about.'

'Fuck off, you cunt. Out with it.'

'I—'

'Out! Don't you want to get back to the Ussher?'

'I do!'

'Then read the fucking room and own up to your past and admit your mother killed herself while you were offline in Manitoba! Admit that when you finally checked your emails and saw you missed her funeral, you withdrew into Camland and your nonsensical narrative theory!'

His sudden sobriety is shocking. His bombshell, however, isn't. Because every word of it is true.

Then he flicks Alt-*Dwelobnik* open to Cian Scanlon's 'Manitoba Dreaming'.

'But here she is. So stop prevaricating, comrade. It's about time. Please.'

Then an alarm clock clangs and makes us both jump and the Pale Fella digs speedily in his cavernous cowl-pocket. He retrieves a mechanical clock and boops it on the head. Then he sets it on the table and smashes it with a bare fist.

'Gourds'n'roll, baby! Let's fucking go!' he says.

Then he sweeps the clock shards into the fire and leaps out of his chair. He fumbles for the door and bolts into the darkness.

And with that, as quick as he came in, the fucker's gone.

So I guess there's nothing left to do but acknowledge the ghost of my poor mother.

Manitoba Dreaming

Unfortunately, yes, it's true.

My mother hanged herself while I was offline in Manitoba.

What else is there to say?

Should I include the grisly details? Or say it was Ger who found her? That Nick, oblivious, was at a friend's that evening and didn't hear of our mother's death until morning?

If I struggle with the specifics of this period, it's because of where I was when my mother took her own life. I can't discuss Canada with the same conviction that I discuss Ireland. Basic descriptions about the place – summations, verdicts, snapshots, verities, lies – take an age to formulate because of the facts that presuppose them.

The facts being that I miss my dead mother and I treated her awfully for years and I was an outright fool to think she never loved me.

So I'm sorry, Mam. I am. But not sorry enough to patch up things up with Ger.

The story is well known. All of Westmeath by now has heard it. I didn't hear it until later, much later, but it goes something like this.

A one, a two, a one two—

Sorry.

Levity is all I know.

If I didn't laugh I'd cry.

No, really.

Anne-Marie and Ger Walton haven't heard from Darren in a month. He's somewhere in Canada. He *was* in Nova Scotia but now no one knows where he's at. He said he was moving to New Brunswick. Did he go to New Brunswick? Who knows. He lies a lot. The emergency number he provided is for an old colleague named Reginald, who knows even less than anyone in Westmeath. He's useless.

Weeks pass without word.

There's a missing persons report and a dozen social media posts. Have you seen this man? Accompanied by his beautifully chiselled face.

Nobody's seen him.

Worry grows.

Then one day in February, Ger's at work, Nick's at school. Nick goes to his pal Fintan's once school's out at Coláiste Mhuire. They're fifteen. At Fintan's, they each enjoy a bounce on Finn's caged trampoline. They snap their crushes, eat Bolognese. They watch three episodes of *Breaking Bad*.

Ger works late at his practice. Everyone on the phone begins with 'Any word on Darren?' He's staying late because he knows Nick's not at home. There's no rush to get back; no panic for dinner, no scramble for piano lessons.

Ger locks up around seven and heads home.

In the driveway, shortly after, his Mercedes rolls on gravel as if flattening thousands of crisps. He looks across the fields, at the darkness of the midlands, and sees the shade of trees whose twigs are loudly waving.

The front door isn't locked. Which, to be honest is peculiar. Last year there was a break-in and Anne-Marie's Golf was stolen (Ger never wanted a Golf for this exact reason) and the door's been locked ever since.

Inside, all is dark. Not even a lamp is on. Ger closes the door, tosses his keys in the dish. He flicks on the light. The house is immaculate, the tiles gleam. There's not a dot of lint on the stairs. The ceiling corners are free of cobwebs.

But in the middle is Anne-Marie, who dangles from the balustrade of the L-shaped staircase. Her palms are open, her face blue. She wears ice-green chinos, a white crew neck, freshwater pearls. She is barefoot.

Ger tries to cut her down. Both from the ground and the upper floor.

After ten minutes he gives up.

Then he rings the emergency services.

I know all this because, once heard, it stays with you.

Could I have prevented my mother's suicide? Perhaps.

Did I try to? No.

Am I guilty? You fucking bet.

I was punished. Even now, as I stack these pages in the hovel, I continue to be punished. Everything that's happened since has been an exercise in flagellation.

But initially it wasn't bad.

It was kind of nice, actually.

*

Hear me out.

I flew to Winnipeg in January and got a VIA Rail to Churchill. I stood outside and lit a cigarette and thought, Holy fuck, that's cold. I saw ice peaks and snow dunes and dirt roads and half-ton trucks. I taught English at the Earl of York. I have no idea how I got the job. But I think I was an all right pedagogue. Most of the students thought I was a Newf. That is, a Newfoundlander. Eventually I stopped correcting them and I went along with the joke. I said mudder and fadder, said b'ys instead of boys. It was fitting. Other Canadianisms had already encroached on my lingo: I said right on, said eh, said buddy instead of your man.

In short, I assimilated.

And life was good because I was accounted for and phoneless and the money I made was decent. I chilled out and saw polar bears. I walked. I read books. I drank and talked to locals. I saved for something I knew I'd need when the time inevitably came.

And b'y, it came.

I was three months into my digital detox when I caved.

Since I got there, everyone at school had been badgering me to buy a phone. I told them I didn't need it. I was in school each day at nine and everyone knew where I lived. Why bother with a phone or a computer? Had they known how liberating it was to live without texts and emails they would probably have followed suit. But they didn't. So it was just me on my phoneless island. And I loved it.

When I say I caved, it wasn't that I bought a phone. I stayed strong. Resilient. Stoic. But I did log into my inbox just to see if I had any emails.

This was in April. How I caved.

I had no friends in Ireland, so I expected nothing more than stray notes from my family. The normal messages of spite, the updates, the how-you-doings.

And what I got was …
Yeah.
There's nothing to say.

I missed my mother's funeral because I was offline in Manitoba. The first thing I read was an email from my father. It was dated February 29. An officious and official letter. A photocopy, actually, of his own bonded paper, with the practice letterhead on top and his signature at the bottom. He had tried to get in touch. By phone, email, the lot. I never answered. My mother was buried on the first day of February. I was no longer welcome in Kinnegad. I was banished.

Fuck, I thought. Holy, I thought. Holy fucking lemon-noodle circumference ghost, I thought.

It was too early for anger, too soon for sadness.

The attendant emotion was something for which I still don't have a name. Looking back, I can only say it was an extreme type of confusion laced with love and energy and suspicion.

And that I uncoiled.

That's a good way of putting it, so I'll say it again.

I uncoiled.

My internal knots unfurled, there was a disentanglement, an ironing out.

It was wild.

It was almost fun.

All of that pent-up malaise I mentioned earlier? The desire for fame? The vacillations? The hate-waves I received from everyone I knew, followed by lulls in which people were genuinely decent and kind? All of that was gone and everything was love. I was free. I was devastated, yes, that my mother was dead and buried. But she was here in Manitoba.

I felt her, could almost see her. She was light and she was in me. She was burning. Pure. Effulgent. And the only thing I was suspicious of was why, oh mother, why couldn't I have felt like this all the time? Why couldn't you die all the time, Mam?

Then I knew.

This was her gift. This internal radiance and clarity for which she died in order to give me. To push me forward. To illumine the road. Her spirit. There was a reason? This was it and here we were.

In Churchill, Manitoba.

My mother and me.

At peace.

The light was so strong, both inside my classroom and within me, that I struggled to sit still by the in-class desktop. Thank god my students were on lunch. I was jittery. But so alive.

Then Anne-Marie appeared at the desk nearest my own.

'Hello, lovey,' she said. She waved, smiled.

I cried.

Then she told me what to do.

I went to the principal and said I had to leave immediately. She couldn't agree more. We hugged before I left.

I packed my bags and caught the next plane to Winnipeg. When I heard I was getting a bereavement discount I clenched my fist. I punched the air.

'Life's a beautiful thing, Betsy,' I said to the airline assistant.

'Stacey,' my mother whispered in my ear.

'Stacey! Of course. Please forgive my slippage.'

'That's quite all right, Mr Walton.'

I took my ticket.

It was strange. My mother was beside me, then she wasn't, then she was. She was constantly in and out of view. But even so she was always within me, coming and going. Like a bad case of the hiccups.

But she wasn't in the ground. (My father never told me where she was buried.) She was here. In Manitoba. With me. At peace.

On the plane I looked at the snowy Canadian Shield and in the clouds I knew that I was hurtling towards my destiny.

In Winnipeg I realised that destiny by not going back to Ireland. My mother didn't want that. No. She did not. But I couldn't remember her plan. So I turned to her and asked her.

'What're we doing again, Mam?'

'Buying a Pontiac, lovey.'

I nodded.

She was so wise.

'I've always wanted a Pontiac.'

'I know, lovey. And you'll get one.'

It was sorted.

I took a taxi into the city and booked a motel and grabbed a beer. Then I consulted Kijiji and quickly found my Pontiac Grand Am.

2.2-litre engine. Manual transmission. Aubergine grey. A real beauty of a car. The asking price was three thousand dollars. When I saw it the next day, I knew that it was for her I'd been saving.

It was for her, always for her, in the beginning it was all for her.

We hit the road, my mother and me. It was special. The best. I loved her.

We were on the Trans-Canada Highway, moving east, in a light snow. The Ontario border was near. I had no idea where we were going.

'Of course you do,' my mother said.

'Toronto?' I said.

'Hah! Do you think I came back from the dead, my love, for twelve-dollar beers and those *ginormous* squirrels?'

'No, Mam. I know why.'

'Tell me, love.'

'You came back for me.'

'Exactly! Watch your speed, lovey. Those crafty Mounties are in the medians.'

'Sorry.'

I cut my speed back to 100.

'We're going to Nova Scotia,' my mother said, 'to murder Hannah.'

'*Murder*?'

'Did I say murder? Ha ha ha! I meant *thank*.'

She really did say 'Ha ha ha!'

'Thank Hannah?' I said.

'Yessum.'

'Hannah McAllister?'

'Your one herself.'

'Who stole my shoes? My baby-blue Vans?'

'That was Kyle, sweetie. When will— Slow the hell down!'

Somehow I was already back at 140. I apologised and cut it back.

'We're thanking Hannah for giving you the light.'

'But *you* gave me the light, Mam.'

I could see it all around us. Especially out in front, where it took the form of a low and yellow sun. It was dawn. How long had we been driving? I didn't care. But it would take at least three days to get to Nova Scotia.

'True, my love. But Hannah diagnosed the *need* for this light, remember?'

I felt like a baby.

'I don't follow.'

'That's okay. Just remember it's the same light that you'll use to start the Pyre of Camland.'

'Mother of Jupity, you're in on Project Pikerowave too?'

She knew everything.

Gourd City, Scanlon, the dossier. She talked for hours. In the end she pulled up her sleeve and there it was too: the gourd tat, the calabash, on the corner of her wrist.

I was missing out.

So we pulled off the highway and in a Thunder Bay mall, with my dead mother by my side, I got my first tattoo.

A pink calabash.

Then I bought twenty CDs because I was tiring of Nickelback on the radio. For company, now, I had Dean Brody and Shania Twain and Rush and Blue Rodeo. Along with five packets of Belmonts and ten identical crew necks I bought to give to people once I got back to Nova Scotia.

Then we hit the road once more.

My mother was proud of me for buying her cigarettes. I told her to think nothing of it. We came down towards Sudbury listening to Blue Rodeo's greatest hits. By the time we got to Ottawa I was in love with Jim Cuddy. The sun went to sleep behind us. The land was flat as a runway. We stopped only for food and petrol and sleep and cigarettes.

I ate a million Timbits.

I smoked a billion darts.

My mother came in and out of view.

I listened and cried with joy.

She wasn't there in person, of course, only there in spirit. Even then I knew that. But her spirit was so strong that none of that really mattered. In these moments we cared like we had never done before. Like we had always dreamed of doing, but could never bring ourselves to do. In our lifetime there had always been a barrier between us. As though we were at a level crossing, which we continually tried to overleap but never could, which was the saddest part.

Now however, it was gone and we were one. There was an oncoming locomotive, sure, we saw and heard it. Toot toot! But none of that mattered because the only thing between us now was love.

We had always been exceptional at ignoring approaching trains.

*

An hour from the New Brunswick border I identified the curious feeling. It was the same I felt the evening I fucked Laird.

'Laird is gone, lovey. He's dead. You're alive. So act like it, you know? *Yodel* for christ's sake. Go ahead. Yodel.'

So I yodelled. And I didn't question when my mother began to speak like a North American.

'Laird was nothing,' she continued. 'I was everything. Do you understand? You're with *me* now. On the road to Nova Scotia.'

'*Oui c'est vrai, ma mere.*'

'Bin the French, lovey. It doesn't suit your cheekbones.'

'*Ceart go leor.*'

'The Irish too.'

'Fine.'

'There you go.'

We were back.

But Anne-Marie wasn't finished with Laird. She reminded me of his pumpkin tea box, which I hadn't thought of in almost four years.

'What about it?' I said.

'It was the first of many gourds.'

'So?'

'Laird was warning you, Darren. He was a parabolic figure.'

I couldn't tell if she was talking about mathematics or parables.

'The latter, lovey. But both work because of the three-dimensional narrative. Laird got lost in the labyrinth. But you won't. Because you're strong. You're not going to be another gourd casualty, are you?'

'No, Mam.'

'That's right. You're— Slow the christ *down*!'

I complied.

'You're going to piece everything together. Aren't you?'

'I am.'

'And you'll never give up.'

'I won't.'

'And you'll study the patterns and always be faithful to Camland and your theory.'

'I will.'

'Because remember Simone's prophecy? Autumn 2017 is closer than you think, lovey. Write your piece before the summer's close. Write it in August, submit it in September.'

I can't tell you how good it was to finally have a sidekick again.

'And here's the ticket, lovey. Which you've been seeking most of your life.'

I looked in the rear-view mirror, where there were peachy strokes of cloud.

'Camland is whatever you want it to be, so long as your ideas there are whimsical. That's all that matters. The same applies for your narrative theory. Okay? Will you remember that?'

'I will, Mam.'

'Great. But on that note, I've got to go. I don't want to, but I've no choice.'

'Why?'

'Because I'm a queen bee and it's illegal to import my kind into Nova Scotia.'

This was true.

'I understand, Mam.'

'All my love to Hannah. And to you. I love you, Darren.'

'I love you, Mam.'

Then just outside Edmundston, while I was doing 130, my mother unclipped her belt buckle and dove out the passenger door.

I haven't seen or heard from her since.

And I doubt I ever will.

But the love lingered. And then some. I just felt so fucking good. I wanted to punch a horse in the face, to piggyback across Canada. Both of which could happen, I knew they could, I could do anything.

And to prove it, I pulled off in Moncton and bought fived iced cappuccinos and twenty donuts and gave the Tims worker a free crew neck. Then I pulled into Canadian Tire and went straight to the back of the shop. To the hunting gear and camp chairs. Then I moseyed to the glass counter, on which I rested a sweaty palm, and I looked the clerk in the goatee and I chirpily said:

'Buddy, I hate fishing.'

'Then I won't sell you no rods.'

'Matter of fact, I'm starting early.'

'Early how?'

'Hunting season.'

'Ah. Smart man.'

'More than just a looker, kid.'

The man was probably twice my age.

'Then what can I do you for?'

'A new rifle.'

'Sure thing.' Then he dead-eyed my facial hair, which I'll admit was unsightly, because I hadn't shaved in days and had a real asscrack of a beard. 'Just need to see your PAL before we get started.'

'My *pal*? I'm a lone wolf, brother. Do I look like I got friends to you?'

'No – your PAL. Possession and Acquisition Licence. For firearms.'

'Oh *that*. Afraid it's at home, chief.'

'Then *I'm* afraid I can't help you.'

The bastard.

I wanted to curse him right there and then, but he was so polite and welcoming that I just couldn't do it. So I took a deep hit of my iced capp and sucked the boyo until it was finished: until the entire Canadian Tire was awash with slurps and unease. Then I knocked on the glass cabinet and gave my friend a finger-bang of approval.

'Keep up the good work, comrade. Santa's watching.'

Then I got back into my Pontiac and moved speedily for Nova Scotia.

I didn't *actually* want a gun. I just wanted to see if I could buy one. To prove I could do it and could do anything I wanted. And the funny thing is that when I failed, my omnipotence didn't take so much as a dent. I felt better than I did before, I turned the music up louder. I *screamed* along to Blue Rodeo, whose every lyric I now knew. Then I crossed the border for Nova Scotia, Canada's Atlantic Playground, where I was reminded by a sign that the importation of honey bees was prohibited in the province.

And there it was.

Home.

I had changed. I knew that. My mother's lightness, which Hannah ostensibly instigated, had changed me for the better, had transformed me so that I could feel at home anywhere, anytime. But I felt especially so in Nova Scotia at that moment.

The setting sun behind me cast a golden-hour glow in every direction. On the highway tar and vehicles. On the yellow and white lines and the nearby colonies of spruce. I felt so fucking alive I rolled down the windows and I hollered at the car beside me and slapped the roof of my car. My cigarette went flying but I didn't give a damn. The adjacent car was a Corolla. Inside were a family of four and a goofy-looking retriever and the father looked at me sideways as I overtook his car. I gave him a thumbs up. He was wearing Ray Bans and a button shirt and had long, luscious hair that was pushed back with a ball cap. He didn't understand how happy I was to see him. I could tell by the way he waved. So I slapped the roof of my car again and hollered sensible words this time.

'I'm driving a Pontiac, baby!'

Then he got the picture.

I accelerated and drove on. I fumbled for another cigarette. I took a drag and I swear it was the best cigarette I've ever had.

Shortly after I was distracted by a sign for a hotel waterslide. No: a hotel *with* a waterslide. What a terrific idea! I was tempted to stop in and swim. But I kept my cool and stuck to my plans and burrowed deeper into the province. I was going to Truro. Or Churro, as Hannah said it. I was going to the Hub of Nova Scotia.

I read the signs along the way, though I can't remember their order. It was something like:

Oxford – Blueberry Capital of Canada!

Springhill – You Should See Us Now!

Amherst – Home of the Slide!

In any case, along the Cobequid Pass I ate a Boston cream and the custard trickled down my wrist until it pooled stickily in my palm.

I lapped it up like lakewater.

In Truro I didn't waste any time.

I abandoned my car on Prince Street, where I ran to Hannah's rental. I couldn't remember the street but I vaguely recalled the whereabouts.

A few ducks and turns later, I was there. I knocked and breathed.

And there she was.

Only at the doorstep, it wasn't Hannah.

It was Hannah's *mother*.

'You're … the Irish boy, yes?'

'I came to say thank you.'

'Well I— That's very kind.'

'For the light.'

'Oh … You shouldn't have.'

Hannah appeared.

'Wally?'

'Your services have been wondrous, Hannah.'

'Services?' the mother said.

'On account of them I'm cleansed.'

The mother sniffed the air.

'I'm not so sure about that, hon.'

'You look *awful*, Wally,' Hannah said.

I put a finger in the air to mystify the mood, then walked back to my Pontiac to retrieve their gifts. I took out the remaining ice capp and the donuts and the crew necks and I placed them on their lawn with the grace of a maître d'.

'A peace offering,' I said.

Then I climbed back into my Pontiac and turned the key and drove away. I waved at them while I did so and they waved right on back. As though I had just stayed for dinner and they were sad to see me go but they knew, deep down, they would see me again soon.

April, April, April.

I didn't want to go back to Ireland, so what else was there to do?

To go back to Halifax, of course, which is exactly where I was headed.

I took the 102 and cruised my way there lovingly.

Brookfield. Stewiacke. Mastodon Ridge. The Shubenacadie river. East Hants. (We Live It!) A giant field in which a giant maple, though not in bloom, was most certainly Living It. I cried with joy and christened it the Tree of Life.

Thereafter to Enfield. Fall River. Dartmouth. To the Angus L. Macdonald Bridge stretching over Halifax Harbour.

And halfway across the structure I knew I had made the right decision. The traffic, moving slowly, was almost at a standstill. I looked around, admired the view. The iron cables held tight. Above me the Canadian flag flapped. Birds swooped. Tail lights flashed. And below us, in the distance, the harbour reflected city lights, all glinting blue and golds.

I revved the engine as much as I could. I was just so fucking happy now that I was home.

'Woohoo!' I cheered.

I wiped away my tears.

Then I put in Shania and blared along to 'Man! I Feel Like a Woman!'

I was on Quinpool in no time. There I filled up the Pontiac. At my old workplace, no less.

'Holy fuck, bud. Where'd you get the wheels?' Isaac said.

I began to fill him in, but after a sentence he interrupted me.

'Buddy … we were getting all sorts of crazy calls? From your folks? They didn't know where you'd gone?'

'Zack? It's okay.' I was the only person who called him Zack. He didn't approve but I didn't care. The name suited him. 'I've spoken to my mother since and everything's fine.'

'You've … spoken to your mother?'

'I have, yes.'

'And how is she?'

'She's fine, totally fine, never been better. Did you speak with her?'

Then he looked at me a moment and I thought he was going to die. The man was old. Really old. *And* he had no teeth. I didn't want him dying on my hands. It would be far too big a hassle. And such a dampener too.

'Ah, buddy. I think you need to go home.'

'Nonsense! I *am* home. In Nova Scotia!'

I paid for my petrol and bought four litres of milk and a single Jos Louis. Then I changed my mind and got another of the chocolate-cake snacks beloved of petrol stations across Canada.

'Hey, Zack?' I said. 'One Jos Louis – two Jos *Louises*! Ha ha ha!'

I really did say 'Ha ha ha!'

*

Ever the gentleman, Isaac insisted I sleep off what he was calling 'my funk' on his couch.

'But just a night, you hear?'

I didn't sleep, I was beyond sleep. Besides, I had a whole jug of milk and my two Jos Louises to get through. It was the best time. Not least because Isaac's living room had over a thousand miniature cat statues. I paced among their stolid, feline glares for hours, and wondered more than once why Isaac would have all these statues but no cat.

All the while I drank milk and flatulated like a four-year-old.

Then summer passed as summers do.

My second day back in Halifax, however, I visited my old haunt, Radley's on Quinpool.

I walked in for a breakfast beer and a chinwag. I walked out with a sublet and a job.

And shortly after, I crashed.

I slept for a whole week. Then I got back on top with the help of cocaine. After which I was golden and I had the best summer of my life. I didn't write a word. I went to work and I drank and made friends and paid rent.

I didn't get in touch with my father. Or vice versa. I figured he'd find out eventually that I was alive.

I got another calabash tattoo, this time on my lower back. I don't remember getting it. But it's black, or red, or something. I never see it, so I always get confused.

In August I got fired for making money moves. Radley didn't monitor his draft, so whenever my patrons got pints and paid cash, I didn't bother ringing up their drinks and put the money straight into my tip jar. I won't deny it.

But otherwise I got my shit together. I heeded my mother's words. I sold my Pontiac with regret and booked a flight back to Ireland. I found a place to stay for September; a student slum in Dolphin's Barn. It was nasty. But somewhat cheap for Dublin.

More importantly, in August I dropped 50 µgs of acid and wrote 'A Brief History of Camland'.

And when I returned to Ireland, things got better *and* worse.

Z = NaN

I don't recall penning 'Manitoba Dreaming'. That is, if I penned it at all. Did I? Did someone else? Does it matter? But as with the prior pieces, every word of it is true.

If I sound calm, I'm not. I'm just an expert at pretending otherwise.

I get up for another can and discover they're all gone; I'm disappointed to feel I'm not even drunk. There's nothing else to do but to finish reading Alt-*Dwelobnik*, but I procrastinate by throwing more pumpkinettas on the fire. Then I wash my face in the kitchen sink. I look out the window, where I see it's quietly snowing down.

I miss Your Man like I miss my mother. Not enough to say it aloud. But I wonder when he'll be back. I'd love to wake him but I'd feel disingenuous if I yelled up, 'Yoohoo! Your Man!' since it's not his real name.

I go for the shoebox and pilfer another cigarette. They're almost gone too. There are approximately forty left.

I haven't seen the Pale Fella since he smashed the alarm clock a while ago. He was talking shite, obviously, when he said everything's in my head. He was just trying to scare me because he knew he could.

After all – I want to tell him now – if I really were mad, how did I secure funding for my PhD? How have I maintained an independent lifestyle for most of my adult life?

I sink into my camp chair and think of the Irish for 'I'm really tired'.

Tá tuirseach an domhain orm. Or, the tiredness of the world is upon me.

Lighting my cigarette, I look to the shitty A4 page on which the Steps to Illumination remain. I think about throwing Alt-*Dwelobnik* on the fire. I'm surprised, in a way, that I haven't thought of this already. But it wouldn't solve anything. And I'd probably disappoint Your Man. He'd scold me and then I'd be stuck in this hovel with him forever. And though I like him substantially and I think the feeling's mutual, he's only here because he has to be. Because I'm a job for which he's paid.

He doesn't deserve to be stuck with me.

So in a rare moment of selflessness, I open up Alt-*Dwelobnik* to its last piece, to Sophie Confey's 'Begad, Kinnegad!'

Earlier this morning, I thought Alt-*Dwelobnik* would clear up everything. Now, having read most of it, I'm more confused than ever. And, worse, what's to come? When it's finished, will I really go back to the Ussher Library? Will I really be illuminated?

My uncertainty, in the face of these questions, resurrects some residual anxiety. I don't like it, no one would, but in the hope of finding out what the fuck's going on in my life, I read on.

Begad, Kinnegad!

My life has changed little in the past three years. Further deaths, shitty roommates, too much booze, arguments, squabbles.

My underground years.

See how they run.

I came back from Canada in September 2016 with something of a four-month hangover. I flew into Dublin, didn't go back to Westmeath. I went straight to Dolphin's Barn. To Chez Squalor, as I call it.

Yes.

At the time of writing, as I stack these pages in the hovel, I still live there.

But it's got a lot better since. It's no longer a five-bedroom house in which nine people live; there are only six of us now. And we're all reasonably clean.

Reasonably.

Back in the day, however, there were maggots in the bins and a stack of dishes so high it was like we lived in a restaurant kitchen. We even had the mice and the borderline personalities to go with it.

The good thing was that my roomies were all sauce-fiends. All undergrads, too, so I felt a little weird. We bonded over cans and YouTube clips of *Rugrats*. And spliffs and 2C-B and the occasional cap of psilocybin.

Those were the days.

Then on September 9 I did it.

I woke to the latest meme on Twitter, where Shelly Burke of Rhode Island had tweeted a photo of her dad, snoozing in a lawn chair in a Boston Celtics vest, with a ball cap on his face and *War and Peace* under his feet.

Using Tolstoy as a motherfucking footrest was sacrilege, no doubt, but at least Shelly's comment was edifying.

'happy bday leo, poppa burke loves u. you literally raise him up xoxo'.

I re-tweeted it, put aside my phone. And instantly, for Tolstoy, I knew what I had to do.

I submitted 'A Brief History of Camland' for consideration in *Dwelobnik*'s eleventh issue.

I thought Tolstoy's birthday was a good omen.

I was wrong.

Life unfolded as life does. What else would it do? Stand still?

I heeded my mother's words. I never forgot about Camland. But I also had an MPhil to do, so I reread Hegel and his monstrous sentences and, once again, I thought he couldn't write for shit. Then I baffled my lecturers by comparing Philip Roth to Louise Erdrich and, boom, twelve months later I had a master's in the bag.

But among all this I tried to dissolve the hostility between Ger and Nick and Maebh and me. And though I failed to do so – spectacularly, some would say – I could stomach the rejection, because it was around this time I met Moya.

Moya, Moya, Moya.

Professor Moya Nolan, that is, whose erudition and wit, I said long ago, had no rival.

It really didn't.

Gosh. What a winsome face she had. And that stringy orange hair! It was the *exact* material you'd find on a jumbo bag of onions. Then there was her lisp. And her ponchos of many zig-zags. (She remains the only academic I knew who regularly wore ponchos.) During our first thesis session, in which I was expected to talk about *The Counterlife* and Kierkegaard, I cried about my mother and talked, instead, about Camland. Soon Moya said I wasn't making sense, that my sentences were disjointed. Could I slow down? I could. Would I see a medical professional? I wouldn't. I spoke about my lifelong fear of doctors, needles, hospitals. She understood. I blew my nose on my sleeve.

Then we repaired to Kehoe's for a jar and a bag of Manhattan crisps. There we actually talked about literature. But it was the strangest thing. When Moya sipped her pint and nodded along to my words, it was as if she was saying, 'Darren? Your mother's death *wasn't* your fault. You are beautiful and she loved you and I love you too.' She couldn't say this aloud, obviously, because we were just getting to know each other; it was too soon for those words. But when we reached for a crisp and our fingers grazed each other's, I felt an electrical flow of friendship course from her to me, and I knew then I could always count on her support.

After this we pretended our meetings weren't what they were – a healthy form of therapy. Even when I levelled up from the MPhil and started a doctoral thesis titled *Existential Realism and Postwar American Fiction*.

She was the best supervisor I could ask for.

But she just had to go and slide into that Offaly pole, didn't she.

However, to backtrack.

February 2017 was a *time*.

Just listen to it. *February*. A dog coughing up your pair of slippers wouldn't be half as insolent as the word February is. A fricative growl for a fricking god-awful month. And I say this with all respect to any Aquarian who thinks otherwise: it is unequivocally the worst month of the year in the Northern Hemisphere.

In February, you step outside and think, 'Fuck, it's still winter?' But you persevere and go for a walk, where you see only nude trees. So you go, 'Trees? Aren't you ready yet? Show us your damn leaves!' But they don't listen. They laugh at you. Yes, the trees laugh. Meanwhile their leaves snuggle in their buds and roll over in the bed where they spoon their neighbouring brethren; they sing delicate lullabies in which the world is a good place, and with considerable grace they sleep until March or April or, sometimes, even May.

And it's awful.

But that February wasn't the worst, for various delightful reasons. For instance.

I bought a used collection of bolo ties. I got my first Swinging BJ, which is almost identical to a normal BJ, except that the person receiving the blowjob sits in a sex swing while the blower stays on terra firma. And I also received a little email from Olivia O'Shaughnessy.

Yes, her of the wire-brush ponytail and eyes the colour of unripe barley.

And the email was an acceptance for *Dwelobnik*, Issue 11.

Fuck did I flip when I logged into Gmail that day and saw the white banner of new mail and knew instantly what it was, before I even read it. This was no email that regretted to inform me that my submission had been unsuccessful. On the contrary! I was *in*. Everything about Camland was finally paying off.

Celebrations were in order, so I walked down to Blackbird and got hammered on my own, in their cave of candles, craft beer and oversized Jenga.

At its climax I was *so* happy that I bought a round of Sambuca for a random group of Erasmus students. When they told me they didn't want them I sank them all myself. Then I whipped out my phone and murdered my passcode a couple times, until I eventually got it right and I thumbed to my messages and sent a risky text to a risky dude.

And all the text said was:

'?'

And the text was for my father.

The intervening month was weird. I contacted everyone I knew from my Project Pikerowave days – Simone, Maebh, Scanlon, Sophie – and expected them to revel in the ecstasy of my news. Publication in *Dwelobnik* was no joke. Added to which, the issue was a special edition about Camland. Even if I hadn't contacted any of these four since Paedogate, surely by now they could see I wasn't making it all up, or that I was finally a reliable source in whom they could confide Camish intelligence.

But the responses were unusual.

Simone Longford was dead, I learned almost immediately, thanks to the most idiosyncratic out-of-office reply I've ever seen.

It went:

'Hi there, Many thanks for your email. Unfortunately I can't reply right now because I'm dying from oesophageal cancer. All best, Simone.'

Following a skim of RIP.ie – that immoveable cornerstone of Contemporary Irish Death – I confirmed that Simone did indeed die in the autumn of 2015, and that she had been telling the truth when she said, in the Iontas basement, that she wouldn't be around for much longer.

Another impudent bummer.

In the obituary photo, thankfully, her impeccable nails were on display. I had missed them. In this instance they were burgundy, shellac, free from jewels, gorgeous.

So that was Simone.

The others were a mixed satchel. Maebh gave me the seen, Sophie and Scanlon never replied. Did they see my emails? Who knows. Either way, I didn't get it. This was a big deal. A *major* deal. I secretly suspected they were in on it and were keeping silent for reasons I'd uncover later on. Or that they were jealous. But I wasn't worried. I was excited.

All in all, it was a great month, until I followed through on my cryptic texts to Pappa Walton and Young Nick and, a little inebriated, hopped on a 115 for Kinnegad.

I've always felt conflicted about my birthday. Not because I'm anti-ageing or anything. I'm very much pro-ageing. Nor is it that I feel sad about getting older.

Rather it's because I have the same birthday as Michael Haneke.

Because, tell me, how is anyone meant to enjoy a birthday they share with a filmmaker whose debut feature climaxes with a family suicide?

But I try.

And in March 2017 I tried too.

I told myself, weeks previously, that I would return to Kinnegad on my birthday. I didn't tell my father or brother. I wanted it to be a surprise. But I tested the waters, sort of, beforehand with Nick.

'Is this Nicholas Walton of Kinnegad, him of the superlative brain and laconic diction?' I emailed.

His reply came a week later. It was fitting.

'Yes'.

All it said.

Oh, Nick. Terse little Nick.

You're going places.

I swear.

And on March 23, 2017 I was going places too.

I was going home to Kinnegad.

But first I had beverages in Frank Ryan's of Smithfield, where the incense was mighty and the dogs mightier still.

Banal fact: Frank Ryan's remains my favourite doge-friendly establishment in all of Ireland. Mainly because the bar is always pitch-black and some of the flooberts (as I occasionally call dogs) trot around in LED collars and hi-vis vests, so that, from afar, all you see is a constellation in motion, or a tiny construction worker on all fours.

In any case, given the venue, I could hardly see my hands, hardly see my pint. But that didn't stop my pinting.

No, sirree. It didn't.

I had five or six of the boyos, and then, nicely lubricated for an afternoon in Kinnegad, I scurried across the Liffey, whose tide was awfully low. I saw a trolley and a chaise-longue and a lot of green glass. But soon I was where I needed to be.

Steevens' Lane, the Chapelizod Bypass, Heuston Station.

There I crossed the Luas tracks for my bus stop, and I admired the nearby trees, a row of fabulous limes whose buds were threatening to bloom. A leftover rain leapt from their black branches. Behind and underneath them were a smattering of daffodils and a buzzcut lawn and a forecourt for an edifice called Dr Steevens' Hospital. But don't let its title fool you: it's just an administrative building for the

Health Service Executive, as every loyal 115-user knows. Regardless, its custard-yellow façade put me in mind first of ducklings and then of gracious swans and finally of an empress surveying her dwindling empire with a scintilla of resignation, if not unwanted magnanimity.

Fuck, I was drunk.

But I wasn't complaining. Oh no. I was so happy I even whistled. Who knows what. A deep cut from *The Wizard of Oz*, *Cats*, *Phantom*, *Jesus Christ Superstar*, *Hair*, maybe?

Probably not. I hate musicals.

But as I took my seat at the bus stop, adjacent to Dr Steevens' Hospital, I gladly surfed the waves of my alcohol-induced lyricism.

On the bus, however, things changed. At Liffey Valley to be precise.

I was listening to *Depression Cherry* by Beach House when the 115 came to a stop and picked up more passengers and I looked out the window at the burrowing motorcars of Ireland.

Then a Dublin Bus caught my attention with its blue and yellow colours and the advertisement on its sideframe, for a film with Michael Cera and Chloë Sevigny and Jordan Peele. For a film called *They Hate You*.

And lo, I remembered my family hate me and always will.

Immediately I saw what would happen if I carried through and went to Kinnegad.

I would get off the bus and walk up the main drag, where I would expect verbal abuse but receive only Howyas. I'd push further up the road to our gated and detached home, inside of which everything would be solemn, sweaty, dim. The dinner table would be set, the radiators roasting. Following a North American beer there would be a fight that Ger would start. First he'd throw words and then mugs and china plates, all of which I'd dodge with the alacrity of a ballerina. 'Relax, lads?' I'd say. 'We're celebrating. No one's dying?' Then Ger and Nick, as expected, would invoke my poor mother. They'd abruptly pin me down and say: 'We'll nail you to the car if it makes you see a doctor!' And underneath their grip, I'd see their real intentions: to murder their oldest son, their only brother. For what's a doctor these days but a euphemism for the morgue? I'd battle my way up, however, and break free of their grasps and, evading their lunges, I'd bail straight for the door. Then I'd run for the 115 and see it pulling off of Main Street. I'd sprint and flag her down and catch it by the hair on my knees. And before long I'd be back in the same place: at the Liffey Valley stop, only on the other side of the road, doing the exact same thing. Listening to Beach House, looking at an advertisement for *They Hate You*.

So no, I decided, I wouldn't see my family that day. I knew what they were up to and they couldn't fool me.

Why?

Because the Dublin Bus advertisements were looking out for me. That's why.

'Thank you, Michael Cera and Chloë Sevigny and Jordan Peele. Thank you, Dublin Bus,' I said.

Then the 115 pulled off and because I had already paid for my fare, I resolved to alight at Maynooth and find the rest of the Camish Crew.

In Maynooth I couldn't find Maebh. I didn't look too hard, admittedly, but after I had cased a couple of pubs and wandered up Carton Avenue, it occurred to me that it was really Scanlon I was after.

And Scanlon …

Hah! Scanlon never failed to amuse me.

I thought I'd surprise him, only this time *I* would supply the mini-muffins. So on the way to his office I waddled into Aldi and bought two boxes. Chocolate-chip and double chocolate. And a cheap bottle of prosecco because it was about time Scanlon and I had a drink together.

I walked by the library and the monument of John Paul II, who somewhat resembled a turtle. It was the cloak, I think, that did it. And his posture: a holy hunch.

Then I scampered across the Lyreen, that little dribble of a tributary, and my feet could hardly keep up with me I was so excited. I pushed deeper into the South Campus. I looked up at the coniferous trees. I admired the neo-Gothic architecture of St Patrick's Cathedral, whose bells were striking twice. I accelerated. I practically ran to Rhetoric House, both of whose doors I threw open with my elbows and my forearms and I bounded up the stairs two if not three at a time.

Then I knocked on Scanlon's door.

But no sooner had he cracked it than he gasped, ever the drama queen, and swiftly jammed it shut.

'Cian! Don't shun an old friend?'

'Go away, Darren.'

'But *Dwelobnik*! They're publishing a special issue. And I'm going to be in it! Surely you heard and got my emails?'

'Oh I *got* your emails. All of them.'

'Then why aren't you excited?'

'Go *away*, Darren. I'll call the guards if you don't leave.'

'That's a bit much, Uncle Scanny.'

'I'm not joking.'

'Really?'

'Really!'

'Oh dear.'

It was quite the dill-scented and toothpick-speared pickle on which I was ensnared.

'I'll go,' I said. 'But I'm leaving the muffins.'

'What? I don't want your muffins, Darren. Please.'

'No, it's okay? They're delicious? Chocolate-chip? Only 294 cal—'

'Take the fucking muffins!'

And that was the last I saw of Scanlon.

*

I was working this whole time, I should say, at The Oxter, a barfly ward on the Crumlin Road, between Dolphin's Barn and Drimnagh. I still work there once a week, despite my IRC funding. Mainly for the chats, the free booze, the endorphins. I'm something of a legend about the house. My patrons called me Razzler Dazzler until I told them to ditch the Daz. Then they did me a solid and re-named me Razzy D. So for the last three years that's all I've been called at The Oxter.

Like Chez Squalour, the bar's cleaned itself up in recent months and years. But during the summer of 2017, while I was writing my MPhil thesis, it was a peculiar Dublin dive.

It was knowingly unpretentious and, for that reason, pretentious. Its clientele had dignity but lacked self-awareness; they all refused to believe that, somewhere in the last decade, they had fucked their lives up. Some wore unironed suits, many had eyes that were tailor-made for infusion pumps. More than one smelled of cloves even though they never drank hot whiskeys.

I flew solo most nights, imbibed almost as much as my patrons.

It was a great source of relief during the clamour of that autumn.

I should have heeded the signs. The summer of 2017 was far too smooth a prelude to be anything other than a warning.

I spent my days then doing five main things: writing an MPhil thesis on existentialism and Philip Roth, preparing my PhD documents under the supervision of Moya Nolan, raising capital at The Oxter, raising hell everywhere else and shooting emails back and forth to Olivia O'Shaughnessy about 'A Brief History of Camland'.

Then in September I submitted my thesis and my IRC application, which, thanks to Moya, was stronger than it should have been. An old batch of undergrads moved out of Chez Squalor, a new batch moved in. I signed another twelve-month lease. Whether or not I received funding for the PhD, I had taken the year out to bartend. I couldn't afford the PhD without the funding.

Then in October 2017 I got my hands on *Dwelobnik*, Issue 11, where I immediately saw there was nothing at all on Camland.

Nothing by Darren Walton.

And needless to say, I came apart.

As with other salient details in my life story, these are not the kind of deets I like to dwell on any longer than I have to.

But you can imagine my fury, my confusion.

For instance.

Why was there nothing of Camland in the issue? With which 'Olivia' had I been conversing all along? What did this mean for the three-dimensional narrative? And why were there voices, in my wardrobe of all places, telling me to chop off my fingers and, with these same fingers, play the *steelpan drums*?

I didn't own a set of steelpan drums! And I sure as fuck wasn't getting any in Dolphin's Barn at nightfall. Besides, my stomach was on fire and my brain wouldn't slow down. I knew there was only one thing that could help.

Saoirse's xannies.

Saoirse was a new roommate, a drama student at UCD. A lapsed Methodist. She told me she had xannies not because she had anxiety but because they were the only way she could hack an acid comedown, the poor baby.

But she was generous. When I knocked on her bedroom door she saw my state and gave me three.

I emailed the usual suspects, to no avail. This time Sophie sent *me* a cease-and-desist. An especially rich development, given Scanlon's similar letter from Cambridge years earlier.

I figured there was nothing else to do but haul ass over at The Oxter.

So that's what I did.

I worked.

I deliberated.

I thought of my dead mother.

I even prayed.

Then I concluded that it was just another test. From whom, I didn't know. But I was being tested by *someone*.

So I persisted, I endured. I got an alumni membership for the Trinity library, since at the time I was in limbo between the MPhil and the PhD. I told myself I'd check the stacks once or twice a week, because one day, I knew, Alt-*Dwelobnik* would show up.

It was just a matter of time.

All I had to do was follow my good buddy Kierkegaard and take a leap of faith.

I became religious for a period to bolster my faith in Alt-*Dwelobnik*, and to prove my plans for fame weren't entirely in vain. I went to Mass for two months. Then, as ever, I bailed.

But thanks to Moya, I was successful in my IRC application. Once the PhD started in September 2018, she coached me through the year. I made disposable friends. I taught tutorials. I did what the IRC still pays me to do: I researched. And while things were improving, I was relying on Moya more than I should have. Four months into my doctoral studies, she said I would have to stop talking about my personal life in our meetings. It was beginning to have an adverse effect on our working relationship. Again she exhorted me to see a professional. Again I said, 'Do you have a fear of doctors, Moya Nolan?'

I didn't think so.

And looking at her, I failed to detect the same level of friendship I first felt in Kehoe's, as we held hands over crisps, and I knew, then, that I could no longer trust her, could no longer rely on her for support.

But a week later I lied and told her I was seeing a professional.

And the next month she was dead.

*

Then Kenneth Connolly, that intransigent bastard, had the audacity to say he'd happily supervise my thesis.

Kenny, Kenny, Kenny.

Whom I'll see very soon, allegedly. And upon whom, it could be said, the fate of my doctoral thesis rests.

What gloriously high stakes! What h

Z = NaN

And that's 'Begad, Kinnegad!', which ends, as I said earlier, mid-sentence, mid-piece. No matter. Everything's there. The biggest gaps have been addressed. And I'll admit I feel less frazzled for doing so.

In any case – at long last – the sun appears in the window, bringing with it a warmth that is too weak as yet to melt all the snow. I set down Alt-*Dwelobnik* and move towards the door, where I see new and old trees, in bloom. There are oaks and larch, firs and peach blossoms, tulips and roses and black-eyed Susans and daffodils.

And on the bark of a hunched oak, I see the etchings once more: VS VS VS.

Who versus whom?

As ever, me versus me.

Then the flowers wilt suddenly and the deciduous leaves die and instantly the foliage is not bright but a light umber. It gyrates and mingles with the slush that is left. The speed at which things change here is frightening. Worse is that the path hither is now gone. The ground still exists, but where the gravel once was is, instead, a canal; it reflects the azure of a clear cirrus morn. There is therefore a rift between the hovel and the trees. I listen for splashes. For birds, children, boats. None sound. But Your Man falls from his spruce and lands on his neat feet, and in his two hands, I see, are two jumbo hot dogs.

He leaps over the canal, enters the hovel, snorting and ruffling. He gives me first dibs.

'Ketchup or mustard, babe?'

I consider.

'English or Dijon?'

'Oh, Dijon. The superior 'sturd.'

'Mustard it is so.'

He proffers my dog.

'Excellent choice, babe. Did you miss you me?'

I did. But I'm gobbling my hot dog when he formulates this question. And I'm a considerate fellow, I never talk with my mouth full, so for a moment there's a silence in which I dance a little. As if to say, 'Hey? My mouth's full and I respect you? So give me a minute, why don't you?' But Your Man doesn't mind. He takes advantage of the silence and starts hoovering his own dog.

My mood has already improved now that we are reunited.

'Delighted to hear it, babe. The feeling's mutual.'

'Sláinte.'

We clink dogs.

'Much happen while I was gone?'

I open my eyes wide as if to say, 'Buddy ...'

Then I fill him in.

'Egomaniacal *and* manipulative? The Pale Fella really said that about me?'

I nod with a full mouth. After I swallow I say:

'But I didn't believe a word.'

'Fantastic, babes. Because he was a test. And you passed!'

I detect a modicum of confusion on my beautifully chiselled face.

'He plays the role of the sot perfectly. Don't you think?'

'He was *acting*?'

'Of course! You don't think he was serious when he said you're currently psychotic in the Ussher Library?'

I pause.

'Or that everything's all in your head?'

I reconsider.

'Or that you were the one to write everything in Alt-*Dwelobnik*?'

'I don't. But if he's wrong, where are the missing pieces? And why are these authors so invested in my history?'

'Missing pieces? You know, babe, sometimes I can't fathom the nonsense you come out with.'

So I throw him Alt-*Dwelobnik* and, with his free hand, he catches it. But he does so in such a way that ketchup slips from his dog. It falls on his shorts, beside his mustard stains and his fly, which I see now is open. Then he gulps the last of his dog and zips himself up, and pats the ketchup down with a scrunch of his tank top. He opens Alt-*Dwelobnkik* with condiment-sticky fingers.

'Holy moly, babe. You're right. Sorry about that?'

I wipe away my lap-crumbs with a supercilious swipe.

'Must be a printing error?' he says. 'A shame, though. You'd have loved it. There was a variation on Jupity, an alternate version of Chez Squalor, an alien sentenced to death for canslaughter.'

'But where— Wait. Canslaughter?'

'Irrelevant, babe. Point is, we're nearing the end of my shift, so there's not much time to get you back to Dublin.'

As I'm still considering the implications of these missing pieces, he wedges Alt-*Dwelobnik* under his oxter. He moves to the counter and snatches the bag of marshmallows, which I completely forgot was there, behind the teabags. They would have been convenient hours ago, when I was starving, prior to the apples and the beers and the hot dogs. Regardless, Your Man rips open the bag and consumes every mallow. Unlike the Pale Fella, he doesn't chew with an open mouth. He's courteous, like me. And I can tell all the while that he's preparing to speak, since he's doing the same shimmy I did moments ago. And when he's finally finished chewing, he reveals his glossy choppers.

There must be exquisite toothpaste in these parts, because his teeth are fucking lovely.

'Normally, babe, when we get to this part of the job, I talk for an hour about unpleasant truths, narrative, selfhood. But today is different, so I'll give you the redacted version. Okay?'

Then, releasing Alt-*Dwelobnik* from his armpit, he catches it with a stealthy hand, and throws it towards me with backspin.

I clasp it with both hands and set it face up on the table.

'I guess,' I say.

'That's not very promising, babe.'

'Okay. I'm ready.'

'Because what I have to say isn't pretty.'

'I'm *ready*.'

'No, really. You won't like it at all. But if you're a good boy, I'll fetch you a treat.'

'I'm not a basset hound.'

'Another astute observation.'

He peers inside his mallow bag as if searching for a prize. Then his eyes return to me.

'The goal of Illumination is twofold. However, it's not either/or. It's both/and. More specifically, it's that you've been both right *and* wrong this whole time. About everything. About Camland, the three-dimensional narrative, Alt-*Dwelobnik*, the lot.'

He's right. I don't like this titbit one iota. But I rationalise.

'That's impossible,' I say.

Then he bonks me on the noggin.

'False dichotomies, babe! The sooner they're out of your system, the better.'

I rub my pate.

'You know, for a friend you're very abusive,' I say.

'It's only because I love you.'

'Hm.'

'So yes. That's Illumination. It doesn't make much sense now, but it will. Very soon.'

I sigh. Now I *do* feel like a basset hound, one in need of a good snooze.

'Why not just tell me outright?'

'I'd love to. But I can't. Because I'm contractually obliged to hold off until after Step Three, until we revise the facts of the present day.'

'Can you at least give me a clue?'

Once again he looks inside his empty marshmallow bag.

'Gerbils,' he says.

'Gerbils?'

He nods.

'Those beautiful burrowers.'

And because this inscrutable clue is not what I was pining for, I wonder if Your Man is in fact telling the truth. Or if the Pale Fella was right when he said that everyone in these parts is just a variation on myself.

'You're your own man, babe. I'm no voice in your head. Sound as you are, I want you gone as much as you want to leave. I'm a salary man, remember. I don't get paid overtime. So recall why you're here. To tell your story, to get back to Dublin, where you'll confront Kenneth Connolly and connect all the dots. For now: here's your treat.'

He upturns the mallow bag and from it drop two things. The first isn't entirely rewarding, it's just a blue BIC biro. But the second thing is pure gold. I give it a whiff, spin her around. I light her up. Inhale. She's just what I needed.

Sativa, baby. A joint.

And not a single crumb of tobacco within her to boot.

'Finish what you started, darling. Take a last step towards Illumination. Your friend there should help.'

Meanwhile, electricals hum and gourds crackle. Outside is frightening change. The sun descends, clouds roll in. Rain, darkness, wind. The seasons bleed into one. We have smoked all our fags, supped all our tea, chombled all our marshmallows, slurped up the poor cans. The canal, now dried up and forlorn, reveals at once its nude contents: broken bikes, water rats, paddles, cadavers. Your Man stands in the doorframe, where he stretches his arms and looks out at the elements, waiting.

I fear my joint will clarify nothing – about Camland, my past, the three-dimensional narrative, Alt-*Dwelobnik* – but I do my best to savour the smoke anyway.

'You're so close, babe,' Your Man says, his back to me. 'So fucking close. You'll have the answer by the doors. I can tell.'

I take a long drag. Then when I exhale I say:

'What doors?'

Your Man turns his head, chuckles, mimics my bafflement.

In the silence I count to eight.

'Let's push off, babes. Let's get the fuck out of here.'

Step Three

Leftyouth Bound

Z = NaN

We leave the hovel behind, looking back as we do. We don't unplug our appliances. Your Man says there's no point, since he'll be back later on. But I bring with me my shoebox and my pen and my Alt-*Dwelobnik*. Your Man insists they're gifts. I am inordinately attached to the container of cigarettes. It's a far better shoebox than the one in which some Kinnegader scrawled my name on a doll's forehead and drove a knife through its belly. This shoebox is a talisman I know I'll cherish forever.

And though I shouldn't be, I'm optimistic. Partly because I've smoked a joint, partly because it's raining. I've always loved the rain, which pools on my scalp and trickles down my face. It's far from a storm in which you've left the washing out; more like being spat on by a thousand hungry Mastiffs. It's gentle. Soothing. Restorative. Kind.

Following the sun, we walk east.

I'm calm. I taste tea and smell candles. The leafless trees around me are too beautiful to talk about. But so imposing too that we have to walk in single file. Otherwise we'd fall into the canal and its detritus. The back of my head tells me that the trees are beautiful because I'm walking towards my death. But the wiser part of me says, 'Ssh, brain? You're stupid.'

'You are very wise to think so, babe,' Your Man says.

I bow.

'Thank you.'

I come close to asking him his name but don't.

We walk.

I see no further signs of life. No animals. Where have they gone? Where are the little creatures, where are the gerbils?

'They're figurative, babe. But forget about them a second and think instead about what we're after.' He pushes through a branch and when it springs back it slaps my face.

'*Ow.*'

I rub my nose.

'Correct! *Power.* Which in the future will belong to the critic. To someone whose understanding of narrative will be so vast that she can manipulate reality whenever she sees fit. To someone who can make sense of a Camland *or* a three-dimensional narrative. But this will occur only when biography, fiction, criticism, theory, philosophy, science – in short, all systems of thought and ways of seeing the world – merge. Do you follow?'

'Not at all.'

'Terrific. I always knew you'd come through.'

I get the impression that he's sticking to his script, so I shut up and rub my nose and look out for further flagrant branches.

Gradually, our path widens and soon we're alongside each other. Without thinking I take his hand. He doesn't resist. He swings it. For a while it's cute, the movement sedate and controlled. But with each dextrous swing he increases his speed, and before long we're swinging with such vehemence that our hand-arc is practically a full 360-degree rotation.

'Okay, that's enough,' I say, patting his shoulder.

The drizzle persists. The arid canal ends in a short wall of bulrushes. Trees cluster. It's day, it's dim.

Your Man leads.

'Step Three of Illumination,' he says. 'Revise the facts of the present day. Recall. Where are we headed?'

'The Ussher Library.'

'That's right. But before that?'

I don't know.

'The doors,' he says.

I forgot about the doors. It must be the marijuana in my system.

The further we walk, the lower the branches become. Twigs tickle our backs, poke our eyes, scrape our heads. Foliage rattles on the forest floor. We duck under one branch only to stoop lower for the next. Soon we're practically on our knees. Then we are on our knees, boring deeper into the thicket. The branches are so numerous that even without leaves they eclipse most of the daylight, so that Your Man and I crawl in near blindness.

Then, almost as quickly as they constricted, the branches clear, their gaps expand. Daylight returns, though only slightly, and I see we're in a clearing big enough for two cars, for two Pontiac Grand Ams. As before, the light is dim, but I can make out what's in front of me.

Two giant doors, at the centre of the clearing.

One's pink, the other's black. They stand idle as ancient monoliths. Above their handles are circular blue stickers. They read, 'Fire door – Keep shut.' The same from the Iontas basement. Before them is a cushioned chair that I recognise from the Ussher Library.

The wind picks up to a moderate gale. The rain is no longer friendly.

Then Your Man points to the pink door, a portion of which looks like it's been clawed with a massive rake, and he raises his smoky voice.

'The Liminal Lair of Logical Conclusions, babe. Where later you'll meet my boss, McDonagh. But now you've facts to revise and Kenneth to see.

Quickly the elements become hostile. The wind fucks us sideways and asunder. Your Man moves the chair so that it's facing the black door. He gestures for me to sit and he grips the stainless steel handle. He tests it. The door's unlocked. But he doesn't open it yet. He breathes heavily. In spite of the storm, I hear smokes on his lungs and his unfit wheezes. Once more I crave fags. My joint is long gone and I'm not even high. I sit down in the chair, keep my shoebox and pen close. I peer inside the lid to see if the pen is still there. It is. Your Man comes behind me and puts a hand on my backrest and we stare at the door in wondrous expectation. He extends a hand. I imagine the door opening at his command. It doesn't. Your Man goes to the door, slaps his face, pulls his hair. He looks awfully coked.

He's strained, there's no way around it.

Then he shouts among the elements:

'Both an augur and a portal, babe! It'll be weird when you find out? Things as you know may never be the same! You might never get over it. But also, you'll be grand? Because you'll be illuminated. You'll see?'

Then he snorts his loudest inhale yet and taps his foot thrice. He hocks a ball of phlegm. The gale passes, the rain stops. There is quiet. He opens the door. Beyond its threshold I see me.

I'm sitting in the Ussher Library, where I scribble wildly at my desk.

Then he turns to me – in the forest – and takes a deep breath and says:

A Torrential Monologue

'Listen carefully now, babes. Follow my orders, okay? The last act awaits, Camland is no one-act play. Leave this world, this one between pages, and go through the door. Reflect on your environs. Where are you? The Ussher Library, where earlier you were enraptured by a pink-and-black book. Do you still have your gifts? Look around you. You do. Only now the shoebox looks a *little* more like your backpack, while Alt-*Dwelobnik* is not unlike *Being and Time*. Your BIC biro's the same. But pack everything up and finish the last of your flask, and slot that away too in your backpack-shaped shoebox, then take the scenic route to Kenneth's death chamber of an office. Jog down the stairs and push out to New Square and circle the tennis courts and follow through to the campanile. Potter along Fellows' Square. Keep going. Don't stop. You'll need carbohydrates before seeing Kenny. So head straight onto Nassau. Cross the road. Shuffle up Dawson. Turn onto Anne and snuggle into Kehoe's. Order a jar, imbibe it, savour the fucking moment. You're in a bar, babe, the best of bars. Tally the crowd. Admire. Bask in the shock of seeing the 115 Guy: he, in other words, whom you regularly see around Dublin, whether in Tower Records or the IFI or at the Ha'penny bus stop, beside the Asian bakery and the vape-cum-sex-shop. Study his glower, his indiscreet fashion. Look for his portable CD player and clip-on earphones. Conceal excitement when you espy them. Propound for the first time that *he* might know of Camland. Rationalise: if everyone significant in your life has been connected in some way with Project Pikerowave, why shouldn't he be? And guess what, babe? You're correct! Slurp Diageo's teat to congratulate yourself, then move to the 115 Guy's table and ask him his name. Produce your BIC biro. Scribble the answer on your palm. "Oisín O'Dea." But don't get carried away. Thank him for his time. Return to your previous table and recall why you're in Kehoe's: to load up on carbohydrates before meeting Kenneth Connolly. So drink your pint and buy three packets of crisps. Cheese and onion, salt and vinegar, and those tiny boyos of bacon fries. Replace a letter – fries to fried – and what do you have? Sophie. That's right. Recall how Sophie Confey of St John's College, Cambridge, fried your brain years ago. Remember that though she deceived you in the past, your reasoning behind "In Defence of Paedos" still stands. Draw on it later to disarm and wound Connolly. Meanwhile, recite it for all in Kehoe's to hear. Stand up on your stool. Take responsibility for its mediocrity, for its status as pure dross. Scream every shit word. You are golden. In control. You absolute babe. Go … In the middle of your recitation, succumb to the bartender's grip as he evicts you from the establishment and throws you onto the cobblestones. Appreciate his efforts to put you on the right path. Thank him. Bid him adieu. Procrastinate no more. Head for the English floor of the Arts Block. Run, babe, run. Once inside the Arts Block, look around, breathe the air and confirm for those who have only scanned the exterior of Trinity's buildings that it's as ghoulish within as it is without. Grant that it smells of vinegar and white pepper. Pound down the dim and undecorated hall and observe the green carpet and bare breeze-block walls, which imbue the air with the atmosphere of a prison. Spot in the vicinity the dregs of the student body. Consider the extent to which people are institutionalised by academia. Suggest that, if this is so, it's on the upper floors of the Arts Block that those in Trinity are incarcerated. Mumble positive affirmations before meeting Connolly. Be excited to talk shop. Manifest greatness. Adopt the full-on fuck-it philosophy to which you said years before you were going to devote the rest of your life, only this time don't read three or four novels unrelated to your studies; make a decision that will impact people of all ages and sizes. Take a leaf out of Maebh's book. Henceforth, when given the opportunity to do something extravagant, do so provided it's unlikely your escapades will lead you to an early grave, a prison, a psych ward or paternity. Cultivate derring-do. Embrace a certain disorder and emulate this spirit during today's sparring session with Connolly. Knock on his door. Listen for the operative phrase by which he vouchsafes permission for any man, woman or child to enter his office. Note there's no answer. Therefore, knock again. Only this time knock the two-bar ostinato from Ravel's *Boléro*. Feel cheated when the door opens as you're commencing the second bar, so that you can't complete the sequence. Frown. Lick the damp from your lips, swallow the saliva in your mouth. Persevere. Nudge forward. See Connolly return to his desk-chair, see his back. Then feel for your gun: narrative incarnate. Smile, for history watches. Stumble into the office and observe Connolly's mouth. Close the door, take your seat. Gather all that you know about Kenneth's past. Acknowledge the absence of sounds and smells in his office. Sink into the vacancy. To it say hello. Concede that on paper you and Connolly are wholly compatible. In a platonic sense, of course. Note the similarities between you. You are both bibliophiles, both reclusive, both obsessed with American literature despite a certain loathing for the New World. You are both prematurely jaded. Wonder then why you never hit it off. Admit Moya's passing in February 2019 was instrumental in your detestation of Kenneth as a human. Do not greet him with a gesture or a platitude. Put it to him that he's a cunt. Voice this concern. Say: "Kenneth? You are a cunt." Log the raising of his brows. Then wonder aloud if he would be willing to share how a Kerryman, of all people, came to be christened Kenneth in the early seventies. Listen to his response. Note the tact in his diction, the concern in the eyes, the suspicion that perhaps you are not quite yourself? Do not satisfy his curiosity. Cross your legs and laugh. Say: "Give me your life story or else I'll yodel, Kenny, I swear." Watch his hands rise in defence and listen to his response, then record mentally that Kenneth, born into a farming family of seven siblings, was the last *babóg* to be thrown from the cosy enclosure of his mother's womb; that Margaret Kitchener, Kenneth's mother, would only relocate to Kerry if she could name her children as she pleased; and that, so it was, Margaret Kitchener of Croydon, London, found herself one day in the remote lassitude of Doolin. Slot away these nuggets in the pantry of your mind, then feign interest on hearing that the Kerry census of 1979 came to have, under the Connolly clan, a Thomasina, an Elizabeth, a William, a Henry, a George, an Anne and finally a little Kenneth. Note that, while farming for Kenneth was a worthwhile enterprise, it was one for which he had no innate proficiency, and that he was consequently the only Connolly to attend university. Note too his confession that he's someone for whom academia is a consolation, a silver if not bronze medal, against his failed ambitions as a novelist. *What?* This is news. Wallow in insecurity. Curse that his fall-back is your life-goal. Ask him again to carry on. Then, tune in to the epiphanic moment at which Kenneth's life changed for the better: on a damp bitch of a day in Norwich, England, when Kenneth was writing towards a Master's at the University of East Anglia, when he came to the horrifying though necessary conclusion that his prose would never match either the scribblings of his peers or the tomes of his teachers. Appreciate that no physical cause elicited this insight. Relish the electrocution. First, the morning roll call, read by a famous British novelist. Then Kenneth's internal question, "Am I on the same level as my peers?" And the immediate response, "No." Respect that he finished his degree and scraped a 2:1 and moved to London, where he wrote promotional material for scaldy nightclubs and bars. Identify with his withdrawal into post-war American fiction, and envy his manifestation of what you wish to do: become an Americanist research professional and, in doing so, cover up not a little of your neuroses and your capacity for self-deception. Consider for the first time the *awful* possibility that you might not wish to be an academic anymore. Oh dear, babes. Oh *dear.* Doubt yourself, move along. Say: "We have become a dishonest species, my mean-spirited Kenny." And in the accompanying silence, be grateful that things are going especially well considering that, to begin with, you called your supervisor a cunt. When he asks you to elaborate, do so with aplomb. But repeat after me, though translate my pronouns. You are golden. In control. You absolute babe. Go … You do not belong here, say to Connolly, but you will never kill yourself for you don't have the courage. You are no Anna Karenina, no Emma Bovary, no Anne-Marie Walton. You are a weak, selfish man at the centre of whom lies a deep-seated instinct towards self-preservation. As if life were a game you were destined to complete and death a cheat code you proudly chose not to use. Did it not exist, this vast will of yours to endure, you would have slit your throat long ago and in your dying eyes you would have seen the biggest of all guns pointed at the Education System until it alighted from its dais as you made peace with all your foes and assimilated with the oppressed and shook off your Tory streaks. Hurrah! But what are you saying? You're talking nonsense, babe. Connolly says as much. He's anxious, he's concerned. "Are you *sure* you're okay, Darren?" he says. You are. But reel it in and repeat the message. You are suspicious of human nature and yet your will bends towards it. "We have become a dishonest species," you say again to Kenneth, who is more worried now than you have ever seen him before. And why? Because you're standing up and over him. When did you stand? Who knows. But well done, babe. I'm proud of you. Your reward? A rotation. A pasture for a final field. Rotate your crops. "Get with it, Kenny," you say. Clap his head, poke his ears. Give his lobes a delicate tug. "You are a cunt, Kenneth. A cunt." Detect his fear as he loudly says: "I don't know what this is about, Darren, but if it's an act it needs to stop!" An act! Good *lord*. Don't despair, babe. Persevere. Though Kenneth be hostile, carry on. He's communicating. But his message is garbled. Translate it, scan, summarise. Appraise his implicit argument about the academy more generally, which is that the academy is all an act, all one big fucking cover-up. For what? Its social powerlessness, of course. For its inability to change society. Yes, that's it! "You're right, Ken!" "About what, Darren?" "About everything!" It's true. So invoke aloud an image: the university as a tower from whose embrasures defending soldiers shoot arrows and throw daggers with which they believe they can quell Ignorance, when in truth the winning strategy is not to fight but to flee, to unsheathe one's sword on whatever castle grounds – whether in Dublin or in Mexico or in Beijing, Lagos, Melbourne – and, naked and sobbing, to perform hara-kiri. Grant that while you are too weak to perform this ceremony yourself, you accept that it's the only solution for the academy. A genuine break with the past, a true tabula rasa. Articulate. "Jesus," you say. "Do I even want to be an academic anymore, Kenny?" You don't know. But look for the answer in Kenneth's Tesco Value glasses: in his eyes as far apart as those of a hammerhead shark. Feel the emotion well within you and the anger his face inspires. Let it metastasise. Hear Kenneth say, "I don't think now is the best time to discuss your thesis, Darren. You seem a little … unwell. Shall we reschedule for next week?" And that does it, it fucking does; his use of "shall" pushes you off the precipice. So flip, fulminate, say: "You are the biggest of all fucks, Kenny. And guess what? *Yours* are the arguments that are uninspired and tenuous, as your lack of doctoral candidates and publication history makes clear. Not mine." Watch his mouth clack, like a ventriloquist puppet's, but steady on, babe. Home in. See the teeth, the lips, the tongue. Think: how *beautiful* would it be were impunity on offer to mash in his head with a mallet or a hurl? Or his legs with a shovel? To hear him whimper and shriek, only for time to rewind so you could do it again? But put away the hypotheticals. After all, this is real. You can do anything, babes. To that end, act. Fulfil your desires: walk away from Kenneth's chair and move to his Library of America shelves. Say, "Never mind, Kenny. I'm sorry. I really am. I don't know what's come over me, but do you mind here if I show you? A little something from *Billy Budd*?" Then take from his shelves the furthest thing from Melville. Take, I don't know, Ursula K. Le Guin. Yes. There she is. Swipe her open and caress her pages with your finger. Saunter back to Kenneth. Protract you shoulder blades, loosen your hips. Listen to his asinine remark. "Wait, that's not *Herman*?" Then loudly rip a page from Le Guin's *City of Illusions* and scrunch the paper in your palm and let it smudge the name of Oisín O'Dea. Snap shut the book and beat the *shite* out of Kenny. You heard me. Beat him, babe. With the hardcover corners, strike his temples and teeth. See the shock setting in. Hear the what-in-the-fucks sounding. Feel the second, the third, the fourth and fifth blows. Shove the page in his mouth and push on his head, then swing your foot round his chair and yank the wheels towards you. Flip, topple, land. Pummel his torso, his ribs! Then remember your tendency towards self-preservation. Suddenly: desist. Remove the bolus from his mouth and rub his belly and click your tongue. Say, "Up you pop, Kenny! I know just the thing for your trouble." Then head back to his shelves and grab a book to make amends, like Richard Wright's later novels, the one that includes *The Outsider*, but take one for yourself too; for all your hard work in the hovel. There: a Didion. *Perfect*. Read the cover. *Collected*—Woah! Feel the blow as Kenneth tackles you to his carpet. Hear his roars, smell his sweat. Respond. Roll and flail. See the madness in his eyes. Fight back, defend yourself. Hear the bellicosity of his soundwaves draw a neighbour from her office. She's new, you don't know her. For that reason, call her Josie. Dr Josie P. Louise. (She's American, hence the initial.) In any case, when she appears, pat yourself and say, "Kenny! What are you *doing*?" See Josie's eyes meet Kenneth's, then stash away your Didion in your backpack-shaped shoebox. Be placid, kind, caring. Study the face of Josie and admit that, since Moya died, they all look the same to you, these malnourished academics. Note her words. "What's going on here, Darren?" Good *god*, she knows your name! "You seem a little … frazzled?" Assure her that, on the contrary, you are the finest you've ever been. To demonstrate, extend your arms and approach her for a hug. But when she resists, back away. Then do the right thing. Juggle. That's right, babes. You heard me. *Now* take Melville and, I don't know, a Hawthorne, and with shocking ambidextrousness juggle the two books. You're a showman, you're in control. But also, you're exhausted. Therefore, take a seat and listen to Kenneth's words. "Are you done now, Darren? Have you *finally* had enough?" Tell him plainly. "Who's to say?" Clock the discretion in his eyes, the phone by his ear, but don't panic, you're fine. Be comfortable, serene. You are incapable of shock. And

Kenneth, fair fucks to him, has not booked you a taxi. He's booked you a *party van* to take you back to Chez Squalor! He's so impressed, too, with your recent revisions that he's giving you *a month off!* Express pleasure, clap your hands, and grab your shoebox-shaped bag. Then allow him and Josie to walk you elsewhere, to the corner of Westland Row, where your party van awaits. Wave to everyone on your stroll there. When you get to the party van, moreover, offer Kenny a knuckle touch. Bump fists and reconcile. Say, "Boosh," or something similar. Observe, at this point, that you feel somewhat tipsy. Let this fact surprise you, since you have only had one pint and a little suppeen of whiskey. Remember then the many cans in the hovel, recall the joint. They must only be kicking in. Exclaim that before you is quite the *commodious* vehicle. Admire the bowler-hatted gentleman who with unctuous professionalism opens the double doors for you. Hop in and clap again. Say, "Woohoo!" Allow the jarvey to buckle your belt. Say it again. "Woo*hoo!*" Cash in on your privilege, cherish your esteem. Take the magnum the jarvey offers you. Gulp heartily. It's champagne! Go for an eye-gander and espy the corner TV, from which noise blares and on which static dances, then feel the ignition spark as the van inches towards to Chez Squalor, whose electricity bill is unpaid and whose rent your landlord's hiking. Then call out to the jarvey, "Excuse me? The tele's broke!" But listen closely: "No, she's grand, Darren. It's the new craze. White noise instead of music. Were you in a club now, that's all you'd hear." Pout your lips in approval. This you didn't know but it doesn't surprise you. It makes complete sense. Nothing shocks you anymore. Not even the loose sheaf of papers that flies before your very eyes. Infer that they came from the cab's thin partition-window. "Some light reading material for you, Darren," says the jarvey. "We've a little ways to go yet." Let the papers fall in your lap and see that the first is a blank page. Estimate nevertheless that there are a hundred pages on your person. Ejaculate, "You silly bean! I won't finish this before Dolphin's Barn." "I'm afraid we can't take you to Chez Squalor, Darren," says the jarvey. "*We?* But why not?" Ignore the growing disquiet you feel under your epidermis. "Because we've to take you home, by way of St Jonathan's." "Come again?" "Leftyouth, Darren. By way of St Jonathan's. Family ties to repair, ideas to put to bed? Anyway, we're getting ahead of ourselves. *Way* ahead of ourselves. Have a read of that thing and a little sup from your magnum and you'll find yourself home in what we trivialise by saying no time, for there can never be a state in which time doesn't exist, you dig?" Repress the unease welling within you because of the shift in the jarvey's sleek diction. Listen, "It's time, Darren. For Illumination. But you haven't laid yourself bare. So do it now. Confront yourself and acknowledge everything in sight. Recognise that there's a part of you that you've always shrugged off. Have a gawk, in other words, at the missing pieces from Alt-*Dwelobnik*." Then let it hit you, that unruly blend of ecstasy and fear that you know oh-so-well. The missing pieces! Turn the page, read its words. "Darren Walton is a spoon." Oh dear, babes. Oh *dear*. This is bad. Not as expected. But it's okay? Keep going. Turn the page and read *its* words. "Darren Walton is a fork." Oh fuck. Oh *deary*. Things are critical, babe. Turn again. Stake all of your hopes on the next page's words. Read, "Darren Walton is a decidedly trivial and mould-ridden piece of unwanted cutlery who should never be used for the consumption of food, hot and cold alike." FUCK! I take it back, babe. I'm sorry. It's all wrong. So very wrong. But skim the rest of the pages, maybe there's a mistake? No? They all liken you to cutlery, eh? Balls. Well since they're not there, the missing pieces, despair. That's right, babe. *Howl*. Keen, grimace, breathe. Then, rein it in. Throw the papers away and watch them hit the window, beyond whose frosted glass you can see a moving shadow. Look closer. Who is it? A friend, a foe? You're not sure. But you think you know the answer. So wipe your eyes again and peer and stare and, this time, *really* see. Then realise it's *me*. That's right, babe: *Your* Man. Waving goodbye to the biggest legend I ever knew.'

The Gorge

When the van doors open I'm ejected into a room that's so blindingly white I need a second to gather my senses. And when I do, the first thing I spot is my shoebox. I pick it up from the floor and look inside. My biro's there, but Alt-*Dwelobnik* isn't.

Instead there are books by Martin Heidegger, Flannery O'Connor and Joan Didion.

Which is strange.

So I turn for the minibus whose jarvey delivered me hence. And she's not there either. Nor is there a road down which a party van hurtles.

There's only a white wall and many rows of tall filing cabinets.

I'm back, then, where I belong.

Where I began.

The Iontas basement.

A trail of melons leads the way to the anteroom. The room is almost as I left it six years ago.

The vegetable patch is there. The posters. GOURD CITY. But there are also gourd splatters on the walls, floor, ceiling. It's an explosive and fresh mess, a detonation of gourds. And what colour too: a red-green hue, concocted possibly from calabashes and watermelons.

The wall displays a message no bigger than my palm. It's written entirely in smears. As I get closer I smell sucrose and realise the message is a couplet.

'Though you were right about everything, Darren, now it is time to leave this filthy warren.'

Below it is a simple instruction.

'Dig.'

Thus I turn to the patch, sink my hand in the soil, and I pull up the magazine with which this fracas began. Nothing's changed. There's the same Camish flag, the same list of contributors. But in it are not the pages I read in the hovel. Nor are the missing pieces. Or any libellous material about my being a fork.

Every piece, however, is identical.

The title is 'About the Author'.

The passage is as follows.

Born and raised in County Kilvan, Justine Heffernan McDonagh is the CEO and founder of Fix Ur Chakras, Kid, a self-help conglomerate that treats psychosis with creative writing. FUCK's ghost-writers work with clients to bring about fix-up novels, story collections, screenplays and erotic poetry, partly to delineate how their clients' lives fell apart, partly to illustrate how they might piece them back together. For the past three decades, McDonagh has divided her time between Kilvan and Darglar.

Psychosis?

Then from the ceiling, a projector descends, and so too does a screen, on which a title card appears.

'Deus Ex Machina', it says, in plain black and white, with old-school curlicues in the four corners of the screen.

I wait a minute. Nothing happens. So I gather the screen is frozen and I look around for a remote, but all I see are gourd-guts. Then I leave the anteroom for the filing room, where I get such a fright that I both jump and yelp.

For standing in a filing cabinet, looking directly at me, is a woman I partly recognise but can't pinpoint where from. She has the winsome face of Moya, the shaved panel of Maebh, the jewelled fingers of Simone, and the smile—

Mother of Jupity, it's my mother.

'Nope!' she says. 'Guess again, my love.'

But …?

'I said guess *again*!'

So while she climbs out from her filing cabinet and starts walking towards me, I think of another answer. She's wearing a piebald coat and speckled plaid trousers, and on her head is a hat that she can't stop fiddling with. Variegated yet silver, pointy yet soft, it's both a crown and a fool's cap. This woman then – if not my mother – has to be J.H. McDonagh, the God-Princess-Queen who employs Your Man and the Pale Fella. And I, by extension, am not in the Iontas basement, but am rather in the Liminal Lair of Logical Conclusions, the world beyond the pink door in the clearing.

'Correct, love! But most of all, you are *welcome*,' says Justine.

Like Your Man and my mother, she has heterochromatic eyes: one green, one brown. She has the calabash tat on her wrist. So I still think she's my mother, and just to be sure I say:

'You're positive your name isn't Anne-Marie Walton?'

She laughs.

'No, petal. I *told* you. I'm Justine Heffernan McDonagh!'

Then she gives me a hug to apologise. And to make matters worse she smells of shin pads and strawberries. But after our embrace I feel a little better. Then she gently shakes my shoulders.

'Congratulations, however! Not many get this far in the game. Some stay forever. Whether in the forest, the hovel, the gorge or the hospital. But you won't. I know it. So please. Come with me.'

I feel my crotch go clammy at the mention of a hospital.

She runs back to the filing cabinet and dives headlong inside it. When I don't move, her crown-cap pops back up.

'Don't you want to be illuminated, lovey?'

I point to the ceiling, since we're in the Iontas basement.

'Illumination's not that way? In Maynooth?'

'Ha ha ha! First of all, petal, it's Slorn. Not Maynooth! Didn't you study your Camish geography? Didn't you literally read the writing on the anteroom wall?'

I recall.

Though you were right about everything, Darren, now it is time to leave this filthy warren.

'I did. But I'm no longer sure I can trust the ideas in my head.'

'Great! That's the voice of Illumination I hear speaking. Now come. Please. It's urgent.'

She drops down the filing cabinet.

And, reluctantly, I follow.

I emerge at the bottom by Justine's side.

'Where are we?'

'The gorge, silly.'

We're in a damp and open place in which metal burns and soot blows. In which the smell of burned hair besets us from all angles. Clusters of singed trees flail as if in a hurricane. And yet, none of our clothing *or* our hair flops. We wade through a stream that comes

202

up to our ankles. There are stones in my shoes that won't dislodge, despite my kicks. There is a darkness to the air that I've never felt in Ireland.

'Again,' Justine says. 'That's because you're not in Ireland, lovey. You're in Camland, see? Gourds.'

She reaches into the water and retrieves a tiny gourd whose particoloured design complements her coat. The gourd is bigger than a pumpkinetta, though smaller than an apple, and spikey as Your Man's skin. I have no idea what it is. Either way, when Justine's thumbnail pierces its flesh, the gourd issues a torrent of chaos, as if from built-in speakers. I hear human screams, mechanical whistles, automated voices and wind noise:

'IT'S BEEN ALMOST FIVE MONTHS AND STILL I FEEL WEIRD.'

'Fuck me, Justine, what the hell is that?'

'Your mother's suicide note, love. You don't remember?'

'She never left a note.'

'No, silly. *Your* version.'

The gourd continues:

'I'M A BUNDLE OF NERVES, SOMETIMES SHAKING, SOMETIMES NOT. NOW I'M WANDERING AROUND IN PURGATORY WONDERING WHEN THE JIG IS UP.'

Raising the gourd, Justine bites into its spikey flesh, after which the gourd-noises cease.

She chews, swallows, says:

'*Perpetual Comedown.*'

'You're telling me.'

'No, that's what you called it.'

'Called what?'

'Your mother's note! Or the one that you imagined. You submitted it to *Dwelobnik*'s eleventh issue along with "A Brief History of Camland".'

'I did?'

Then she looks at me as if she's trying to count my eyelashes.

'Gosh. You really don't remember, do you?'

I shake my head.

We move on.

'So that's the gorge,' she says. 'And now for the hospital!'

I don't tell her that since I was a gossoon I've been terrified of doctors, so I cling tight to my shoebox and yearn for more cans.

'But because the road there is long,' she continues, 'let us sing some tunes to help keep us cordial.'

Thus we fire up primary-school songs, from the canon of *Alive-O* and *Beo go Deo*, and alternate with each verse. She sings one in English and I, being a gaelscoiler, smash out the other in Irish. It's marvellous. It banishes all anxiety I have. And in what feels like no time we reach our destination: an elevator situated in the centre of the gorge.

Inside, we take a deserved break from singing.

Then Justine tells me about FUCK and answers my question about *John* Heffernan McDonagh.

'Another fine mistake of yours, my love. You wrote something like: "Only a god, his machine rusty in descent, can save us from Camland." And as ever, only a part of you was right. Because there's never been a *John* Heffernan McDonagh. Only a Justine. Wonderful, no?'

'That better not be Illumination.'

'Ha ha ha! You're funny. But it's not. However' – she sniffs the air – 'Illumination is close. I can smell it.'

I sniff too but all I smell is burning.

The elevator dings and opens onto a hospital ward so generic as to resemble a film set. I'm shook, but Justine takes my hand, whereat I'm soothed.

We push on.

Do I belong here?

Am I *safe*?

Judging by the staff, with their scrubs and their scowls and their medical regalia, I'm not. But Justine's presence is so calming that I say nothing of the sort. Besides, she's perky.

'Stephen, Aengus – great to see you're back in action! Cathleen, just *loving* what you've done to the place in my absence!'

We pass a floor administrator, who hands Justine a bunch of papers. Justine thanks her, then conveys the papers to me, with the last page facing up, on which I see dialogue and sluglines.

I think I know what this means, so I flip to the first page to verify.

And I'm right, for the top of the page says, 'Deus Ex Machina – A Short Film by J.H. McDonagh'.

The same from the anteroom in which I stood not long ago.

Justine leads me to a room with a twin bed and a bay window. The view I know well but I haven't seen in a long time. The grass is the colour of wet spinach, the clouds are low enough to get lost in. I see birds. We're ten storeys high. At the very least.

What we're looking at are the stalwart Irish midlands. We're looking at Westmeath.

'No, lovey. *Leftyouth*. Don't you remember anything? The jarvey's words? Leftyouth, by way of St Jonathan's?'

I nod.

She points to the screenplay.

'Have you learned your lines at least?'

'Uh ...'

With the shoebox under my arm, I skim through the script. It's all nonsense about clowns and giant books. Then there's my dad playing a fucking tin whistle.

'Your *lines*, petal. Have you learned them?'

I look up.

'No. I have no idea what you're talking about.'

She sighs.

'We worked for *ages* on this. You really don't remember?'

'Also no.'

'Fuck.' She looks around. 'Fuck!' She clenches her fingers. 'FUCK!' She smashes the bed with closed fists.

'Mam, st—'

'I'm not your fucking mother! So *please* shut up with that.'

Her profanity takes me by surprise. My mother never swore.

'I'm sorry,' I say.

Mumbling something incoherent, she comes closer and rolls up her sleeves.

'We're going to be all right, son. We're all co-writers anyway, despite what the page says. Your Man, the Pale Fella, myself, you. Your mother, rest her soul, even had something to say. You were proud of the result, even if it was a little literary. We were going for drama but you didn't quite grab it. Something about an aversion of yours to spy movies and exposition? No matter. Mere quibbles.'

'But I don't *write* screenplays. I write academia!'

'*Do* you? I think you're done with that, petal. Because look around you. Where the hell are we?'

Outside, a hundred pigeons shit on a hundred huffing heads.

'We're *still* in a world where your z-value is Not a Number,' she says.

I keep quiet because I feel it's required of me.

Then she takes my script and shoves it inside the shoebox, after which she reaches for my waist and immediately wrangles me from my jumper.

'All off, Darren. Time for your final role.'

Strange as her request is, I don't feel I have a choice. And because her aura's so enchanting I'm as calm as I've ever been. And yet, despite my equanimity, I fear nothing in my life will ever make sense again.

'I could say you're in Ireland, petal, I could say you're in Camland. I could say many things. Hundreds, thousands, millions. Because that's the aim of the game, here at FUCK – infinite alternatives.'

I hand her my jeans, T-shirt, socks.

'Thanking you.'

She crams them into the shoebox.

'You see, both Your Man and the Pale Fella were correct. As were you. On the one hand, you were right all along. On the other, your ideas are a dead end. And until you recognise false dichotomies for what they are, your life will remain fucked. Here, throw this on.'

She puts a hospital gown over my arms and around my uncouth body.

'You'll play your final part perfectly, whether or not you know your lines. The best ones are all improvised anyway, are they not? M'ere. In you pop.'

I climb under the bedsheets and no longer feel afraid of doctors, needles, nurses.

Justine continues.

'With Camland, unfortunately, your thinking was always black and white.' She wheels over an infusion pump and takes my arm and rubs it. 'For you, Camland was a story in which no character had an arc, in which there were no second and third acts. But for Scanlon, you said, it was a play whose foundation was self-growth. Let me ask you a question, though. Why can't the two of you be right? Why can't the two of you be wrong? Why, instead of an A and B, can't there be a C and a D and so on, until we run out of letters?'

She pierces my arm but I don't feel a thing.

'False dichotomies, lovey. They're all over your life story. Go back to the first one. Mascu-femininity. A Grade-A dyad if ever I saw one.'

The return of this ancient idea takes me by surprise. I no longer remember what it means, other than that my intentions at the time came from a good place.

'But that was the opposite of a dichotomy?' I say. 'That was ... two things coming together and as a result ... good things happening?'

'My point exactly, petal. You haven't a clue! And so Your Man's right again. You don't have control over the ideas in your head, the ones that most excite you, and as a result you can't explain them. So tell me – and think seriously about this next question.'

She sneezes.

'Bless you.'

'Thank you. You have lovely manners. Did you know that? Your mother taught you well.'

'But you're my m—'

'I'm not your mother, Darren. I'm sorry. I really am. But back to my question.'

She blinks.

'If you don't have control over the ideas in your head, might it be possible they're not your ideas? Might it be possible that they belong, I don't know, to another person, another group? And *that* group gave you these ideas?'

I hear myself ask in the voice of a confused child:

'But you and Your Man said I was right all along?'

'Yes, but Camland and the three-dimensional narrative are not *your* ideas, lovey. They never belonged to you.'

'Then whose *are* they?'

She fiddles with the bag attached to my infusion pump, after which she presses a button.

'Cambridge University's.'

Then my serenity fades, my fear returns, and the pump beeps so loudly it sounds like it's wailing.

'Remember Your Man's clue? His little gerbils from earlier? A guinea pig, Darren. That's all you are. You've been a guinea pig your whole life. No: for seven years. For Cambridge University. Their scholars have been working on the *craziest* of books, whose ideas they tested out, initially, on you.'

Whether it's the drugs in my system, or the nature of this bombshell, speech is no longer something I possess.

'You want to ask, "How?" And it's a very good question. But bring everything to its logical conclusion, petal, and you'll find the answer is Scanlon, the answer is Maebh, the answer is Simone, Sophie, everyone. Everybody you encountered at Maynooth is complicit. They're all working for Cambridge. How else could Cambridge have infiltrated your system?'

This is not a good feeling swirling around in my stomach.

'And guess what, lovey? That's it, that's the kicker. Happy Illumination Day! Just as you were right all along, so Camland's a dead end! And just as you've been a Cambridge guinea pig for years, so you've be— Actually, that's the last piece of the puzzle. I can't finish that clause yet.'

I blink furiously as if to ask why the fuck not.

'Don't give me those eyes, lovey. The answer's in the script. You'll know *real* soon. I promise.'

The infusion pump screams louder.

What the fuck's in the bag?

'It's okay, petal. Just for show. They're all props. Your speech will return in a jiff, too, I swear. This is your destiny, remember?'

Then she returns to the shoebox and picks up the screenplay and waves it around her head like a little white flag.

'This is how you claw yourself back, how you return somewhat to normal. And don't worry about your lines? I mean it: you'll be fine. When the action starts, you'll know what to do. That's how it is with everyone who's been in your shoes.'

But why?

'Ah, Darren. You're lovely, you really are. We'll miss you when you're gone. The simple answer is this: not everything needs a reason, an explanation, an exegesis. Some mysteries are better off as they are, obscure, impenetrable. But because you asked, you'll receive. We're doing this so that you can make amends with your family and all those you've burned over the past seven years. We're doing it so that you might live a decent life, if not adopt a new worldview. So to that end, let's get to it.'

She fetches my shoebox and heads for the door.

'All my clients get what they want, Darren. *Everything*. And remember when, in Nova Scotia, you said you wanted an extreme point from which you might never come back? Well, this is it. Only it won't be as you thought. So I advise you, when we start the next and last session in approximately thirty seconds, to think of the good things. Your positive desires. The life-affirmers. They'll help pull you through.'

With four fingers, she toodaloos.

'You're on your own now, lovey. All the same, see you soon. And thank you, I mean it, for using FUCK's services.'

The door closes.

And she's gone.

Then from the corridor I hear the jumping pumpkins from earlier. Instantly I'm hooked on their beat. I'm bopping and grooving so much I start chanting – in my head, since I'm mute – a modified version of the gourd-couplet from earlier. But only the second line so that it complements the pumpkins. She's triplety, baby. She's allegro, she's fine.

One ti ta, two ti ta, three ti ta, four ti.

Now it is time to leave this filthy warren.

1   <u>**TITLE:**</u>

Deus Ex Machina – A Film by Justine Heffernan McDonagh.

2   <u>**INT. HOSPITAL – DAY – OCTOBER 15, 2019**</u>

DARREN (25), recumbent though not supine, awakes in a bed.

Beside him – an infusion pump.

Its wires spool downward into Darren's right forearm. It beeps.

He's alone.

In the far corner of the room is a small patch of soil, above which is a laminated poster of a buffalo gourd.

<u>ANGLE ON:</u>

The wallpaper around Darren, which he jumps out of bed to inspect.

It's a smooth, velvety red, and depicts a microwave in the shape of a fish.

That's right.

It's a Pikerowave.

A gentle hiss comes from a radiator. Weirdly, it's nearer the ceiling than the floor.

NARRATOR (O.S.)
Darren is overly warm despite that heat rises.

Though Darren hears the mid-Atlantic voice, he doesn't recognise it. Accordingly, he's alarmed.

He looks up at the radiators, scratches the wallpaper, walks around. Tries the door. Looks for clues. There are none.

NARRATOR (O.S.)
Darren is overly warm despite what he's wearing.

Darren surveys his hospital gown.

With a crash, the room's only door opens.

Before Darren is GER WALTON (57), his father. He has a fine mop of hair for someone so close to sixty. His chin strap, however, negates his otherwise fine looks.

He holds a microphone in one hand. In the other, a tin whistle.

He slams the door shut. He speaks. He's the narrator.

GER
Darren has never been so lost.

DARREN
Stop acting the clown, dad. 'Mon.

GER
He has never gone so astray.

DARREN
Dad, for fuck's sake, you don't talk like this.

GER (OVER)
His writerly conquest has been unplugged. By whom he
knows not. All he knows—

DARREN (OVER)
You're from fucking Cork! Stop!

GER (CONT'D)
—is that it has been unplugged and he can't see a socket.
Indeed, there isn't one in the whole room.

Ger lowers the tin whistle. He points first to the infusion pump,
onto which Darren's hand remains clasped, and then to:

The cord, limp on the floor;

The plug, also beside it;

The corners of the room, in which there are no sockets.

Yet the pump steadily beeps.

Darren rips the wires from his arm.

ANGLE ON:

Ger moving towards the curtains, which he pulls back.

<u>INSERT</u>:

An enormous field, with a body of water on the horizon.

While he and Ger take in the view, Ger plays the opening notes of 'Hot Cross Buns' on the tin whistle. Darren is just about to say something when:

The door crashes again and into the room come:

THREE CLOWN-GARBED DOCTORS, who are—

SOPHIE CONFEY (44), CIAN SCANLON (49) and OLIVIA O'SHAUGHNESSY (46).

<u>INSERT</u>:

SCANLON'S DOSSIER—

'in which staff at St Jonathan's Hospital are required by law to wear clown costumes on the job'.

Then Darren knows where he is:

St Jonathan's Hospital, Camland.

To break the silence, Ger bangs out an air on his trusty tin whistle, which Darren smacks from his hand and it cracks the windowpane.

Cian Scanlon steps forward.

SCANLON
Think everything over, Darren. The answer's right
simple?

OLIVIA
Cian's right, honey. So simple. Who's the only person that
can save you?

Darren is sick of his ideas. He doesn't want an elucidation. He
wants boring old Ireland, where he might decompress from this
whirlwind.

SOPHIE
Hear Justine out, Darren, then we'll get you back pronto.

Everyone trades eye contact, in expectation. Then:

JUSTINE HEFFERNAN MCDONAGH (49) sashays through
the door.

She wears a piebald jacket and a diadem-fool's cap and speckled
plaid trousers and killer green wedges.

She picks up the shoebox, which she shoves towards Darren.

When he takes it in the stomach, however—

3   EXT. THE FOREST – TWILIGHT – CONT'D

—he's winded. But he's also back where he found himself earlier,
by Your Man's hovel, holding the shoebox.

Justine is the sole person beside him.

215

JUSTINE
We're changing your viewpoint, lovey. Understand?

Darren, looking around, is pissed.

DARREN
Where are we?

JUSTINE
Just another field of yours. Nothing wild, you know?

Darren opens the shoebox.

When he does—

4 **EXT. PUNT – CAMBRIDGE – DAY – CONT'D**

—he's in a punt, in Cambridge. Justine punts. Students cycle.
Tourists take photos.

A golden glow comes from the shoebox, which Justine closes shut.

JUSTINE
My colleagues and I at Cambridge—

DARREN
I thought you worked for FUCK?

She bonks him.

DARREN
Ow.

JUSTINE (OVER)
False dichotomies, petal! But as I was saying, my
colleagues and I at Cambridge have assembled a Theory
of Everything, at the centre of which lies you. There
never was a Bloomsbury book deal for Camland, never
a UCD convention. They were all just ways to get you
thinking. And you were just an experiment to see if
our ideas could stick. And they did! But don't look so
confused. Everything's in the shoebox.

Which she thereupon snatches and chucks overboard. Darren
reaches for it, screams.

When the book flies off-screen, however—

5 INT. IONTAS ANTEROOM – DAY – CONT'D

—we cut to the basement anteroom, where Darren catches the
box and takes in his surroundings, which are as we last saw them.

Vegetable patch, gourd-smears, posters, melon trail.

JUSTINE
Normally I just spell it out for our clients. But you're a big
boy, Darren. You can put seven and four together. So tell
me – what do you think of Cambridge's Theory of
Everything?

She bends down and scoops up a handful of soil.

DARREN
How the fuck should I know? I haven't read it.

217

JUSTINE
So true!

Then she flings soil into his face. Darren yelps and rubs his eyes.
And as he does so we—

6   **INT. ST JONATHAN'S – DAY – CONT'D**

—match cut back to St Jonathan's, where everything is almost
as it was before, though no one else is there. Only Justine and
Darren, who is shocked, when he opens his eyes, to see he's back
in St Jonathan's.

JUSTINE
My Big ToE.

DARREN
What about your fucking toe?

On his lap is the shoebox.

JUSTINE
No. *My Big ToE.* As in: T – O – E. My Theory of
Everything. You know? Look in the shoebox.

He opens it. Balks. Reaches in and pulls out, somehow, a book
whose dimensions are 1m³.

On the book's cover is J.H. McDonagh, in space, dropkicking the
earth.

The lysergic font reads:

MY BIG ToE – EDITED BY JUSTINE HEFFERNAN
MCDONAGH.

Its spine says Cambridge UP.

Darren estimates there are 8,000 pages.

> JUSTINE
> Read that, lovey, and you're good to fucking go.
> Everything you want to know is in there. The missing
> pieces from Alt-*Dwelobnik*; an extensive history of
> Camland; notes on your general surroundings; everyone's
> involvement in Project Pikerowave; not to mention the
> influence of the three-dimensional narrative on literary
> criticism more generally.

> DARREN
> But none of those ideas are mine, is what you're saying?

> JUSTINE
> True! But pursue that thought. I feel you're almost there …

> DARREN
> Well … it doesn't matter if I was right all along, because my
> ideas were never my own.

> JUSTINE
> This is so exciting! Why not, pet?

> DARREN
> Because even if I was famous one day for the three-
> dimensional narrative, it wouldn't matter because—

JUSTINE
Woohoo! Finish that sentence!

DARREN
—because Cambridge would sue me for plagiarism and I'd
never work again.

Justine produces a party blower and blows it inches from Darren's face.

JUSTINE
That's fucking Jupity, baby! I mean, shit, Illumination!

Darren pouts. He's dejected. He hasn't cried yet in these parts, but he's close to doing so now.

DARREN
This is very sad news, Justine. I'd like to go home please.

JUSTINE
We will, petal. Extremely soon. But first: your consolation.
Do you still have your pen?

Darren looks in the shoebox. His biro is there. He nods.

JUSTINE
Amazing. Let it be the pen, then, with which
you write *Visual Snow*.

Visual Snow?

DARREN
The pen's my prize?

JUSTINE
No, petal. This is.

Justine scurries to the gourd patch, hunkers down. She sinks a hand in the soil and rummages for an age and emerges, after some struggle, with a bundle of yellow notebooks.

JUSTINE
Just a little apology from everyone at Cambridge and FUCK. We'll admit we were excessively hard on you.

They're the same yellow notebooks Darren used while he was a student, in secondary school, at Mullingar's Coláiste Mhuire. Justine dusts off the packaging and hands the bundle to Darren.

JUSTINE
Again, let these be the receptacle for *Visual Snow*.

DARREN
Is that supposed to make sense?

JUSTINE
Not yet. But it will. Meanwhile, everything other than that makes sense, yes?

DARREN
No! Not at all! I am so confused, Justine. There's so much I don't know. And frankly I don't care. Just take me back to Ireland!

This isn't the reaction Justine was hoping for. Nevertheless:

JUSTINE
Very well, Darren. As you wish.

She steps to the window and motions for Darren to join her.

The view is no longer of the Irish midlands. Leftyouth–Westmeath is no more. Instead, the window gives onto an edifice.

Darren scampers to the window to take a better look.

Beyond the building is a river; closer to them, a busy road. There is a buzzcut of a lawn. And the 115 bus stop.

Then it hits him.

It's fucking Dublin.

It's Heuston Station and the Liffey, it's the Chapelizod Bypass. He looks down and sees a row of lime trees the colour of fresh pumpkins.

Then he looks to Justine, who smiles maternally at him, before turning back to the window.

Then the view shifts suddenly and pulses back and forth: at once Leftyouth–Westmeath, now Darglar–Dublin.

Again, Darren knows where he is.

Dr Steevens' Hospital.

But why Dr Steevens'?

DARREN
It isn't even a hospital?

JUSTINE
Come again, pet?

DARREN
Dr Steevens'. Where we are? It's an administrative
building for the HSE.

JUSTINE
Oh, that! Thank god you noticed. I forgot. Ha ha ha!

Darren stares out the window at the shape-shifting view.

JUSTINE
Remember that unfinished clause I mentioned earlier?

DARREN
Remind me again.

JUSTINE
About how the Pale Fella was right even though you
didn't believe him?

A most unfriendly feeling swims around Darren's stomach.

JUSTINE (CONT'D)
Well … yeah: just as Your Man was right, the Pale Fella was
right too. And just as you were onto something all along, your
ideas were also a dead end. And lastly, just as you've been a
Cambridge guinea pig for seven years – and it's they who've

been putting thoughts in your head – you've also been
clinically delusional for the same amount of time.

Darren stares out the window as though he hasn't heard Justine's
words.

JUSTINE
You're psychotic, Darren, it's simple. This isn't
Dr Steevens'. It's the building next door that was founded by
Jonathan Swift. It's St Pat's.

Darren doesn't believe her. He knows, like the Pale Fella, she's
just trying to scare him. To what end, it doesn't matter. All the
same:

DARREN
But this view of Heuston could only ever be from Dr
Steevens'? So how the fuck am I in St Pat's?

The laziest of gods, Justine shrugs.

JUSTINE
Beats me, comrade. It's your life. But for now – a closing
question. Did you get what you wanted in life,
like, for real?

Darren has never heard a more stupid question in his life.

DARREN
No!

                            JUSTINE
        Very well. But what was it you wanted, like, for real?

Darren has to think about it. He thinks very hard.

Thankfully, he's saved by a knock on the door.

A NURSE (30s) pops her head in.

                            NURSE
        Sorry, miss? I'm afraid your stay is up. Darren needs
        his rest. Feel free to come back tomorrow, however.

Justine moves for the door.

                            JUSTINE
                Oh that won't be necessary.

At the threshold, she turns around for a final word.

                        JUSTINE (CONT'D)
        Goodbye, lovey. Until next time. Your new steps are the
        easiest. Read *My Big ToE*, mind your shoebox, and most
            importantly, write *Visual Snow*.

And with that, Darren is alone.

He looks out the window at Leftyouth–Westmeath, at Darglar–
Dublin, and mulls over Justine's stupid question.

What was it you wanted, like, for real?

And after an hour of staring, an hour of thinking, the only honest answer he has is:

a mother's love.

My Big ToE

When I come to, the first thing I notice is that I'm in a bed that smells of lavender and whose sheets are white and thin.

It's a twin.

The room is big.

My right foot is outside the bed. Not on the floor, but atop the sheets. My toenails all need a cut. Not least my big toe's.

There are windows, high and sashed, and radiators, low and on.

I'm alone. There's beeping. But it doesn't belong to an infusion pump. It comes from the window, beyond which I hear construction workers and active machinery. Behind me are the unmistakable squeaks of plimsolls on tile.

So yeah. Call it intuition, clairvoyance. Call it whatever the fuck you want.

But I know I'm in a hospital.

And my plastic gown proves it.

'Boom,' I say to no one. 'I was right all along.'

Either seconds or hours later, I see books on my bedside table.

Being and Time, Flannery O'Connor, and an LoA Didion I don't remember buying, but which I'm pumped to see.

Aces, I think. More Didion. Hell yeah.

I don't see either Alt-*Dwelobnik* or *My Big ToE*. But they'll show up.

It's only when I reach out for Didion that I realise I'm groggy, as if my blood were made of treacle and I were underwater to boot.

All the same, I grab the book. I pull it close and open it. I see the Library of America logo, and under that, a name.

K CONNOLLY, it says.

Then I remember.

I'm in St Patrick's Hospital. Or so Nurse Navan tells me.

I ask if he knows of Jonathan Swift. Then I ask on the hour if he knows that good ol' Jonathan funded this very hospital. He laughs every time. He's a good guy, Nurse Navan.

I call him Nurse Navan because he told me that's where he's from. But I stop when he tells me he only *lives* in Navan and that he's actually from Moneygall, County Offaly, so after that I just call him Gavin.

I ask the doctors about Alt-*Dwelobnik* and *My Big ToE*. I ask them about Camland but none of them know shit. But they all tell me I'm really interesting, and are sincere about it too.

'Would you like to stay longer?' they say.

And just because they're so nice, I tell them, thank you, yes, I would.

'Great,' says the fiftieth doctor I've seen in two days. 'Because the longest you can stay in this capacity is seven nights. Even with private insurance. Since you were involuntarily committed.'

This is news to me.

'Cool.'

'Do you remember why you were committed?'

'Unfortunately.'

'And why was that?'

'Because I bet the shite out of Connolly.'

'Terrific, Darren. Thank you.' She scribbles onto her clipboard as if drawing loop-the-loops, and mutters all the while: 'Patient ... is ... responsive.'

But, lest she return it, I refrain from telling the truth about my Didion.

The nurses are altruistic because they appear at the right time. The doctors are inconsiderate because they arrive at three in the morning. But I look out for myself by voicing my complaints.

'What are you at?' I say. 'It's three in the morning?'

'It's five in the afternoon, Darren.'

I tut.

'That's no excuse.'

They write this down. But I imagine that what they're actually doodling are pornographic caricatures in which I lounge in wingback chairs and chomp on unlit cigars.

These, of course, are reveries. Just little things to busy myself until the next bowl of Rice Krispies comes my way.

Or *My Big ToE*. Or the missing chapters from Alt-*Dwelobnik*.

A boy can dream.

Soon, however, they arrive.

Yes.

My father and Nick.

'Well isn't this *fantastic*?' I say. 'All of the lads? Back in action once again?'

My father still hasn't shaved his god-awful chinstrap. He says nothing. Nor does Nick. So I have to do all the talking while Poppa Walton glowers like the twentieth-century man that he is.

Do they blame me for my mother's death? Are they finally finished grieving? Are they sad, troubled, happy, angry that I'm here, in the bughouse? Are they trying to make amends, or trying to rub it in? Is their presence in the room an admission of love or hate?

I'd like answers to these questions but I intuit it's too early. Instead I smell the room, and I deliver another remark to which I wouldn't mind an answer.

'The bang of incense off you is shocking, Ger. You just in from Mass?'

He keeps silent.

It's then I realise that while *I'm* totally willing to patch things up with my family, Ger isn't quite there yet, and that he might need more time. Our first conversations, therefore, will most likely be one-sided. Which is allowed, I guess.

I make a mental note to go easy on him.

But in the aftermath I remember something, and I say:

'Tell me, Ger. Can you play the tin whistle?'

Eventually we make up and the reconciliation is too easy. So much so that I'm suspicious. Something's awry. Perhaps Cambridge reached out to Ger? Maybe they forced him to come to my aide? Perhaps my father, in this drawn-out affair, has as little agency as *me*? In any case, I push my worries aside, and when Ger finally starts talking, he fills in a few gaps.

He was here, he tells me, on October 15, the night I was committed. I was full of wild talk about forests and books. He was convinced for a while I was in love with a hedgehog.

I laugh until Ger tells me it's no laughing matter. It was Serious.

'With a capital-S, boy. And it remains Serious now. You might have been having fun in your world, with its … magical trees and codes—'

'Mother of Jupity, Ger, the trees!'

I remember the carvings.

VS VS VS.

'—but it was no laughing matter sorting Kenneth's settlement fee.'

'The etchings on the trees, Ger! VS. The *code*!'

'What now, Darren?'

'It stood for *Visual Snow*.'

'Which means?'

I consider.

'I don't actually know yet.'

Now he does laugh. He nods.

'Good lad.'

We're getting there.

The great thing about antipsychotics is that, under their influence, I no longer feel like Ger and Nick hate me at all. The bad thing about antipsychotics is that they'll never erase the fact that I've been a guinea pig all my life, and that the ideas in my head have never been my own, and that academic fame will never be mine.

But Kenneth could have pressed charges. So things could be worse.

He had a burst lip, my father tells me, and a cracked rib and many bruises. Ger was onto him by October 16. He offered an immediate settlement fee. However, I am now legally required, he says, to stay ten metres away from Kenneth. So I guess I'm not returning the Didion.

And that was, what, a week ago?

As in the forest, so here.

Time runs slower yet quicker than it does normally.

Most days Ger brings in an *Indo* even though I ask for a *Times*.

Today I learn that a twenty-seven-year-old man was killed last night when he drove off a ravine near the Kildare–Meath border. Authorities say there are no signs of suspicious behaviour.

There's a photo of the individual. He looks somewhat familiar.

Then I realise who he is.

Ah, *no*.

It's the 115 Guy.

Otherwise known as Oisín O'Dea.

There have been too many preventable deaths on the road hither.

I say as much to my psychiatrist, Dr Gallagher, the gatekeeper to whom I'm expected to tell my story in exchange for a diagnosis, a prescription and a ticket to ride the fresh hell out of here.

'Laird. Simone. My mother. Moya. And now Oisín O'Dea,' I say.

'It's difficult,' Dr Gallagher says. She has a platinum-blonde bob and eyes the colour of sapphires. 'You're having a really hard time.'

'I *am*, Dr Gallagher. Thank you for noticing that.'

She insisted at first I call her Lindsay, but I like the formality of her title now I'm over my phobia of doctors. Now that I'll never *be* a doctor.

'But you know what?' I say.

'What, Darren?'

'There's a consolation.'

'What's that?'

'I got a good joke out of my troubles.'

'Did you? Can I hear it?'

I think about it. Then I deliver:

'You ever hear about the PhD dropout who became an academic superstar?'

She humours me by thinking about it.

'No.'

I smile.

'Me neither.'

Before long it's November and the chestnut leaves are falling and pooling alongside the sycamore slush that's in the garden.

I spend most of my time yammering to medical staff, and patients, until my paranoia overwhelms me and I pop a pill.

But Custodian Ciarán – I'm really stuck for nicknames here; I don't know what it is, the regime? – is a great source of conversation. We either talk of hurling or I rant at him. I like to tell him he's missing the point.

'You're missing the point, Ciarán! My ideas were *inserted* in my brain by Cambridge University. So no matter how ingenious they are, I'll never be famous for them. Because if I *was*, Cambridge would sue me for plagiarism. Sneaky, huh?'

'Quite the predicament, boss.'

'And sure, maybe in three or four years when *My Big ToE* comes out, I'll get a special commendation in the acknowledgements or something. But true academic fame will never be mine. I've been a guinea pig all along and, I see now, *that's* what Your Man and the Pale Fella and Justine were talking about, when they started our little game of Illumination. That's the last word. But I have to fight back, you know? I can't sit down and die?'

Custodian Ciarán shrugs. He gets uncomfortable when I talk for too long like this. So I change the subject and ask if he thinks he could out-puck me.

And he does.

So we agree we must go for a puckabout some day.

Dr Gallagher is more sympathetic, if suggestive.

'What if you wrote about your experiences and feelings?' she says.

'Oh please. You *have* to listen to me, Dr Gallagher. No one will ever pay me to do so. Any other great ideas?'

'I meant a diary, Darren.'

Then I change the subject and ask if she's heard any more of *My Big ToE*.

She hasn't.

I defy modern medical science.

Dr Gallagher and others don't know what to make of me. They draw complex family trees and timelines for my story. They pore over every tiny detail. They see several diagnoses and yet they can't commit to any.

They see psychosis and mania predominately.

And yet look at my beautifully chiselled face? I'm as healthy as can be.

Bipolar with rapid cycling is how they diagnose my mother. I knew this all my life but I never liked to say it. In my younger and more imbecilic years, I thought that if I ignored it, it would simply go away.

I have a genetic predisposition, then, to manic depression, they say. But they don't see major depressive episodes. There's dysphoria, sure, during my time in Nova Scotia. And in Chez Squalor. And quite possibly now. But my so-called 'first-episode psychosis' goes back to November 2013, when I first visited Gourd City.

(I have since intuited that this visit arose when Simone Longford paid Maebh €500 to take me to the Iontas basement, after which Maebh signed an NDA to say she'd never utter a word of it again.)

They say I have the psychosis of schizophrenia and the mania of bipolar. They have a label for it too. They say we're looking at schizoaffective disorder.

But again – I'm not buying it.

To their labels I say, No.

I baffle them with my lucidity and my command of the English language. With my impeccable self-care and my exceptional mushroom and cheese omelettes.

234

We agree it doesn't add up.

But little of my story does.

So.

What to do?

As part of my 'recovery' program I contact those I've 'hurt' and I apologise for my actions and I tell them how I'm doing. I write long handwritten letters in fountain-pen ink and I trust the medical staff to deliver my messages safely. I have no phone or computer, no communication with the outside world. It's very similar to Manitoba.

And within a week, I have printout emails from Scanlon and Sophie Confey.

They are glad to hear from me. And are sorry I'm unwell. Scanlon doesn't mention the mini-muffins, Sophie doesn't mention *My Big ToE*. But it's okay. I forgive them. I'm not sure why, but I do.

I'll see them another day, we'll grab a beer, and all will be well.

The following afternoon I'm in a session with Dr Gallagher when we get word of an emergency; some narcissist in another ward has just tried to kill himself.

Dr Gallagher, of course, pops out.

'I'll be just a moment,' she says.

So to busy myself I snoop around her office, and in her desk drawer I find the wildest fucking things: my letters to Scanlon and Sophie, which Dr Gallagher told me she posted.

I'm disappointed, because I hoped Scanlon and Sophie would frame them when they got them. But I guess Dr Gallagher just took a photo of the letters and emailed them instead. And I don't really blame her; she saved on the packaging and postage.

Then I hear shoe-leather on tiles and bring my snooping to an end. I shove the drawer close and take my seat and laugh. I chortle at new logic that's materialised in my brain.

Cian Scanlon and Sophie Confey both work for Cambridge, and Cambridge have knowledge of my every thought and action. So Scanlon and Sophie don't *need* to see my letters to know that they exist.

That's why Dr Gallagher never posted them.

How *stupid* am I!

The matter is so hilarious that I can't stop laughing even when Dr Gallagher returns. She asks what's so funny, and when I calm down I dry my eyes and lie.

'Oh nothing,' I say. 'Just something an old friend said once, long ago.'

Then one morning an old friend does in fact appear.

'Hello sunshine,' she says.

I look up from my bed.

'Maebh!'

She stays at its foot and, even so, smells amazing. Like a meadow. Or cut grass.

I'm so happy to see her I don't even ask about her contribution to Alt-*Dwelobnik*. Or her role in *My Big ToE*. Or if she's breaking her NDA by being here to begin with.

But I learn, funnily enough, that I texted her during my fugue state of October 15. All my text said was: 'In Gourds We Trust', followed by ten or twelve of the askance-eye emojis. She tells me she acclimatised to these sporadic texts years ago, but that my letter was the first time she felt she could respond.

'So here I am,' she says.

'Here you are. Wow.'

Then we reminisce about Maynooth, and Tiny Palace. I'm confused to hear that her version of events is somewhat at odds with my own. However, once I remember that Maebh's always been a spoofer, I realise that her gross distortion of the facts is just an attempt to cheer me up. So I politely laugh at her jokes. I ask her how she's doing and she tells me she's doing well. She's living in Drumcondra and writing copy for online businesses. Last week she wrote three thousand words on fireplaces.

'Riveting stuff,' I say.

'Don't I know.'

Then I stick out an open palm and I get what I'm looking for.

Two ultra-fast claps, our secret handshake of sorts.

I chuckle, for even today it amuses me more than it should.

After a while we stop talking and are content to say nothing. We share the friendliest of smiles, during whose attendant silence I realise what's missing.

'Any chance of a cocktail, Kealy?'

She tilts her head and deadeyes me.

I raise my hands in defence.

'You're right,' I say. 'Too soon.'

I smile again.

'Missed you, buddy.'

'You too, sunshine. You too.'

Maebh, my father, Nick.

They come regularly. It's nice. They bring encouragement and Crunchies and news from workplaces and schools. I question their motives occasionally, namely why they were so quick to make amends, but on the whole I stick to the script and tell them I'm feeling better.

Before long, it's December. The plan is to leave before Christmas.

I've learned, thanks to Dr Gallagher, that I have many so-called 'delusions'. That my family hate me and always will; this is one of them. I pop a minor tranquiliser when it returns and say, 'Shoo, delusion, shoo. Get the hell out of town. Git. '

In other words, I've got tools.

But the other so-called 'delusions' are much harder to quell. Even with major tranquilisers.

These are my hard-earned truths about Camland and the three-dimensional narrative; those that Cambridge sowed in my brain. Dr Gallagher tries to explain them with references to her own obsession, the psychiatrist's bible, the *DSM-V*.

However, I know better than to believe her.

I'm sorry, Dr Gallagher. I love you, but you're wrong.

Yet she persists.

'One common symptom of psychosis is thought insertion. Or the belief that your thoughts aren't really your own; that they've been inserted into your brain by another person or institution.'

I circle my stomach with an index finger.

'I'm going to stop you right there, Dr Gallagher, because this is not a good feeling you're stirring up inside me.'

'Of course, Darren. We'll leave it there for today.'

I feel like I'm the only person on the planet who's ever felt this way, who's felt so right and wrong simultaneously. This sense of internal rupture isn't easy to deal with. I know the truth because I'm illuminated, and know the truth is dual-sided. On the one hand, I know I was (and perhaps remain) a gerbil for Cambridge University. On the other, I acknowledge the medical staff's truth, which they're so desperate for me to believe, and which is the same as Justine's closing words in St Jonathan's Hospital, the same as the Pale Fella's drunken babble; and it's that I've been clinically delusional for seven years.

But who to believe?

Can both camps be right?

Do I want both to be right?

238

I don't know. I see no solution to the puzzle. Nor a future in which I'll ever come around to my doctors' views. I envision no antipsychotic that could rid me of these headaches.

And so, as with the mispublication of Alt-*Dwelobnik* two years ago, the only thing to do is to follow my buddy Kierkegaard and throw logic to the elements and to take a leap of faith.

Otherwise I'm left with suicide.

And thankfully, I'm not pained enough to end my life just yet.

I leave tomorrow.

Somehow, I know it's time to let my ideas go. To bin them for real this time. Because I can't live as I did for the past seven years. I won't do it again. It's unsustainable. It's … yeah.

I want to get better, whatever that entails. But I don't know if I can. I want to *be* better too. Which is something that really scares me.

I keep looking for the viewpoint that Justine said was imminent.

We leave five days before Christmas.

Maebh picks me up at noon. She's taken the day off work and is driving me to Kinnegad. I'll work with my dad as a clerk until September. My funding's gone, but that's okay. I'm almost certain I don't want to go back to academia anyway. I know what I *don't* want, I think. But what I *do* want is harder to say.

I gather my belongings and say goodbye to Dr Gallagher, to Nurse Navan (AKA Gavin) and to Custodian Ciarán and a whole bunch of other peeps.

Then I buckle up in Maebh's Punto and she pulls onto Steevens' Lane. And though we move in a westward direction, we take a little detour in getting back to Kinnegad.

I know we're in the midlands when there's a boreen and a stone wall that's a thousand years old. That, of course, and the lakes.

The sun is low, the sky is deep. Beyond the blue is the black of space. It's cold. There's hoarfrost and rime even though it's past noon. We see rabbits and foxes in addition to the usual animals – cows and sheep and birds and horses.

Then we're there.

We get out of the car and walk to the gate, which we open with a creak and push up the path.

I look at all the headstones but each looks the same.

Then when I get to my mother's grave it's like looking at my handwriting: it could not and will never be anything but my own.

It's boarded by black marble, decorated with white and grey stones. The headstone is plain, elegant. I read it aloud.

'Here lies Anne-Marie Caroline Walton, beloved mother of two sons, and devoted wife of Ger Walton. May she rest in peace.'

And the years in which she was present in her body.

'1964 to 2016.'

I think of apologising but know the gesture would feel hollow. This is not Manitoba. I am here, she is not. I look around and see firs and hear the chirping of robins. I hold Maebh's hand: I hold my friend Maebh Kealy's hand. There is a quietude to Leitrim I have never appreciated until now, despite the family reunions my mother continually dragged Nick and me to. When I recognised the quiet then, it only ever seemed boring. But today all is different.

Then, when I lay a poinsettia on the grave, I *see* something different.

No.

It can't be?

A sweat claws my skull and I feel my throat flush. I focus on my breathing but the thing doesn't go away. Then my fear crashes over me like a slow-motion tsunami. It's smooth and sublime and as devastating as can be.

For what's there on the grave, among the grey and white stones, but a fucking pumpkinetta.

The desire to scream takes hold. But I don't. I squeeze Maebh's hand.

'Darr— *Ow*. Ease up. What's *wrong*?'

I say nothing. I just stare at the little globule of evil.

'What's wrong, sunshine?'

'Gourds ...'

'You're seeing gourds again?'

'*There*. You can't see that?'

I pick it up. Its texture, size, smell are all the same from the hovel. Were I to eat it, I know, it would shatter my teeth. Or I'd be chewing it for ages, just like the Pale Fella was.

'A pumpkinetta,' I say, dropping it in her palm.

There's a moment in which I know that she sees it. She has to, I'm certain; there's a clear wisp of recognition in her eyes. Then she says:

'It's just a stone, sunshine. You are holding a stone.'

She puts the pumpkinetta in my hand and closes my fingers around it.

'I need to hear you say it.'

'Say what?'

'What I said. That you're holding a stone.'

'Don't be silly.'

'Please. For me?'

My fingers clench the flesh of what I know is a gourd; there isn't a chance I'll ever believe Maebh's lies. But I repeat her words emptily. To keep her happy.

'I'm holding a stone.'

And it's a moment before I open my fingers. But when I do, I see I'm holding a grey stone.

'Gosh. Look at you, Maebh. Maybe I'll start calling you Your One from now on.'

'Excuse me?'

'Long story. I'll fill you in later.'

She laughs.

Then I return the stone to the grave and wave so long to my mother and heave a relieved breath because, at the moment, life's fine.

Then Maebh and I turn and we stroll to her Punto, into which we clamber under the glow of an auspicious sun, and as we drive south-easterly and inhale the surrounding crisp views, I look upon the midlands and remember I'm going home.

Acknowledgements

Gratitude to Yan Ge, Madeleine Keane, Rick O'Shea and everyone at the Irish Writers Centre, without whose Novel Fair this book would still be a Word doc.

Boundless thanks to all at New Island, especially to Aoife K. Walsh and Stephen Reid, both for their belief in *PC* from the earliest stages and for their superlative editorial comments. Thanks also to Caoimhe Fox and Mariel Deegan for steering this book towards publication and beyond; to Neil Burkey and Djinn von Noorden for their scrupulous eyes; and to Jack Smyth for the cover.

Thank you to Paul McVeigh, Jacob Barnes and Ryan Baesemann for early support and words of encouragement, namely while *PC* was still a short story.

Thanks to my pedagogues, from Kilcock to Maynooth, Belfast to Belfield.

Love to my friends and to *PC's* earliest readers: Cian, Eoin, Avril, Charles, Olly, Michael, Ruairí, Laura. Thanks also to my neighbours and relatives and family friends.

Love to Cheryl and Jim: for the housing, sustenance, libations and merriment – before, during and after the genesis of this project. Thanks specifically for the ideal space and setting in which to compose a first draft.

Grá, finally, to my family, and to Laura, for more than I'll ever be able to write on this page.

All remaining errors are my own and/or Darren Walton's.

Z = NaN

Your Man, alone at last, appreciates the quiet close of the door. Its sound echoes through his land with an inquisitive trepidation. He's conflicted because he didn't say goodbye to his last client. But now isn't the time, he knows, to get sentimental. It's time to walk home, eat uncooked rice, throw some gourds on the fire, and start a new book.

As he moves west, he wishes he had a horse. Despite that he has never ridden a horse before. He likes the idea of jumping the canal, on a thoroughbred stallion whom, naturally, he'd name Stephen. He is pleased, therefore, when he spots up ahead a small pony-shaped tree. He has traversed every patch of this hilly realm, but not once has he ever seen this specimen. Its hardwood frame is squat and loping, its leaves are green and in the shape of a teardrop, and from every branch dangles a hardcover book.

Yes.

That's right.

Stepping closer, Your Man sees thirty or so books, all of them wrapped in a yellow dustjacket. All bear stickers that say, 'A *Darglar Dispatch* Book of the Year!'

The book is by Darren Walton.

The book is *Perpetual Comedown*.

'Ah, babes. You were supposed to call it *Visual Snow*! Couldn't you heed the signs on the trees?'

There is no one in sight to whom he utters these words.

Then, sighing, he pulls Darren's book from the branch nearest to him, and it snaps off with ease, the pop pleasures his ears. It's true he needs a new book. Last night he finished Blue Turnip's *Crop Rotation Couples*. Thus he stomps his way home with Darren's book in tow and, whistling, relishes the fact he's off work. For a whole twenty-four hours!

No one, he thinks, can currently take his solitude from him.

And yet, no sooner has he started his journey than Your Man sees a gaunt man drinking out of the canal. He wears a camel-hair coat that's filthy and torn. Your Man doesn't wish to be seen, so he hides behind a beech lest he be sucked into more work. But when the gaunt man pulls back, Your Man recognises who he is.

'Andrew *Laird*?'

Turning, Laird sees Your Man's ruby spikes.

'Good *god*, what in heaven are you?'

'Don't mind me, pal. What the fuck are *you* here for?'

'Precisely what I wished to talk to someone about! I've been wandering for *years* and I have no idea where I am. Could you kindly point me in a direction, then, where I ought to be going?'

Your Man shakes his head. He just can't believe it.

'I don't get paid enough for this, Laird. But here.'

He shoves *Perpetual Comedown* into Laird's villainous hands. He was looking forward to reading it, but for reasons into which he's not willing to go any further, he must give the book to Laird to ensure he doesn't have to work overtime. Besides, he feels like he's heard Darren's story before.

'Keep walking,' Your Man says, 'until you find two giant doors. If a Pale Fella approaches you, ignore him. He's full of shite. When you get to the doors, go through the pink one. Find J.H. McDonagh. Then give her this book and tell her I sent you. She'll know what to do. But most of all, Andrew, get the fuck out of my life. Tomorrow's my only day off and I have too much to read. I don't have time to mollycoddle you while you pass through these parts. The nerve of you, honestly, showing up at this time.'

And with that Your Man's off.

He pushes past Laird, in a huff, homeward bound.

Laird, on the other claw, is stationary, though upbeat.

'Godspeed, my friend! Thank you for your services. I'll never forget you!'

Then he sets upon his journey and walks along the canal, in which he doesn't look too deeply and so he doesn't see the bodies. He keeps his eyes in front of him. As a result, he's content. For after seven years of wandering, at last he has an answer! His purpose is to find the doors. *And* he has a saviour in J.H. McDonagh. Not to mention that prickly fellow. Thus he feels a sense of closure wrap around him like a cowl. He wants to celebrate, to drink. He craves a glass of wine. And maybe, he thinks, J.H. will have a drop? Maybe they'll uncork a Pinot and chat for hours later on?

In the meantime, he walks. And feels raindrops on his pate. He looks up at the ceiling and sees a million tiny slits. There are parts of our lives, he thinks, that we willingly patch up, while others must remain porous forever.

He has no idea what this means, or what he's about to encounter.

And, even so, he's not been this happy in years.